D0355589

The Occupation of Joe

The Occupation of Joe

Bill Baynes

Winchester, UK
Washington, USA

First published by Top Hat Books, 2018
Top Hat Books is an imprint of John Hunt Publishing Ltd., No. 3 East St., Alresford,
Hampshire SO24 9EE, UK
office1@jhpbooks.net
www.johnhuntpublishing.com
www.tophat-books.com

For distributor details and how to order please visit the 'Ordering' section on our website.

Text copyright: Bill Baynes 2017

ISBN: 978 1 78535 822 7
978 1 78535 823 4 (ebook)
Library of Congress Control Number: 2017949628

All rights reserved. Except for brief quotations in critical articles or reviews, no part of this
book may be reproduced in any manner without prior written permission from the publishers.

The rights of Bill Baynes as author have been asserted in accordance with the Copyright, Designs and Patents Act 1988.

A CIP catalogue record for this book is available from the British Library.

Design: Stuart Davies

Printed and bound by CPI Group (UK) Ltd, Croydon, CR0 4YY, UK

We operate a distinctive and ethical publishing philosophy in
all areas of our business, from our global network of authors to
production and worldwide distribution.

Also by Bill Baynes

Bunt!
ISBN: 978-098299202-9

1

Isamu

The radio seemed so certain. The voices were so proud, so stirring. The sacred war was going well. It was nearly over. It made his chest swell.

Father would be home soon, Mama promised. He would take them to a bigger place, one with space for Hana-*chan*, who never stopped crying. Mama said the baby was hungry. Who wasn't?

Who isn't?

Six months later and the radio is silent. No good news. No songs to glorify the Emperor. No electricity.

No Father, either. Mama doesn't talk about him anymore. Not since that day a few weeks ago when the young soldier knocked on the door and bowed, his boots caked with mud, and delivered that telegram. That awful telegram.

Now no food.

Mama hasn't eaten in days and she's gone dry. Nothing for Hana-*chan*. No milk and no money to buy any. He has to do something.

Huddled in the corner, his arms around his knees, he looks around the room, murky in the wan light from a single window. Not much remains of their meager belongings.

His stomach hurts.

He watches Mama giving his sister water. Hana-*chan*'s cries don't seem as loud lately. Maybe he's getting used to them.

Mama blows softly on the baby's face. She glances over at him and smiles gently.

"Come sit with us, little man. Warm yourself."

He pushes himself to his feet and shrugs his skinny shoulders. He feels a little shaky.

"I need to move around," he says in his high-pitched voice.

1

"I'll be back in a couple hours."

Mama purses her lips and nods. "Be careful."

He clatters down the rickety stairs. He crosses the shabby lobby and pauses, watching the street through the warped glass in the ornamental door. It's empty. It's early, barely light.

He turns up the collar on his thin shirt and steps outside, his bare feet in sandals. The October wind is icy. Unusual. It's often warm this time of year. It still smells like smoke.

Better than baby shit.

He looks around carefully. No rats. No dogs.

Does he dare?

He has to. Mama, she has to take care of the baby. It's up to him to find some food. He has to go now.

He sets out across the ruins. It's the first time since that night six months ago when he and Mama dashed across the streets, dodging the burning buildings and the desperate neighbors. He's stayed close to home since then.

He used to roam as far as the docks, exploring and playing with the other children, but nothing looks familiar now. He keeps to the side of the dirt road, away from the holes and piles, trying not to draw notice. He trots past the temple his family used to attend. Two walls are standing, a smashed triangle of roof leaning against one of them.

That pile there, the one with the charred rickshaw, that was the Sasaki family. He remembers the mother trying to save the baby strapped to her back, the padding smoldering, then her trousers flaming, her husband's too. They fell where they stood.

He tries to concentrate on what he's doing, but he can't keep the images from flashing across his mind.

The bombing was bad enough. Hearing the sirens every night, the drone of the big planes. Never knowing the target. Waiting for the explosions.

Then the fire, the night it happened everywhere, the entire city filled with live sparks and bits of burning wood and paper.

It felt like it was raining fire.

Bursts of light flashed high in the sky and fell to earth, whistling. A huge glow spread over the city, showing the big planes, flying low, their wings slicing through columns of smoke rising from the ground.

The voice blaring through the intercoms was calm as always. "Take shelter. Do not panic. Take shelter. More attacks coming."

People stood in their gardens and watched, spellbound by the spectacle. Red puffs of anti-aircraft guns sent dotted red lines across the sky. Thousands of cylinders dropped with a rushing sound like a downpour and then exploded into flames. Frail wooden houses bloomed alight.

He realizes he's been running. He stops and leans over, hands on knees, breathing hard, fiery images flooding his memory.

He spots a group of bigger boys in the distance. He heard they ran in packs now. He hides behind a water barrel outside the husk of a house.

That night, the night of the fires, he remembers he jumped in a water barrel because of the intense heat. He splashed Mama and his sister until they were soaked.

Then they ran across the streets, where telegraph poles and overhead trolley wires fell in tangles, him pulling his mother by the arm, her other arm holding the infant.

Today the wind is stiff, but nothing like the night of the fires. He saw a burning plank sail through the air and hit a man, killing him instantly. Fanned by heavy gusts, the flames spread as fast as people could flee.

Coils of black, choking smoke surrounded them, but there were unexpected open spots, where he and Mama coughed and gulped the good air. They couldn't hear each other over the roar of the firestorm.

Now the breeze blows the cinders like dirty snow over the acres of crumbled structures and charred rubble. When the bigger boys pass out of sight, he hurries past a shuttered shopping district. He waves to Mrs. Kuraki, mother of his friend Kenji, who died of the burns he suffered that night.

Isamu steers clear of the homeless in their lean-tos built against standing walls or collapsed roofs. He stays away from the few remaining brick or block structures, fearing the desperate people who shelter in the hollowed-out interiors.

He cuts across another block of desolation, girders in gestures of supplication sticking out of the blackened ground. His feet are completely gray.

He catches sight of the Sumida and trots over the bridge spanning the river. When he looks down, he sees the thousands of bodies that clotted the water that night, living people splashing among the burned and drowned, a putrid stew of ash and flesh. The ghastly smell – will it ever leave? He retches and runs.

The next thing he knows he pulls up again, gasping. He's missed the last minute or two, caught up in what took place months ago.

After that night, he refused to leave the room for more than a few minutes. Stunned and numb, he spent those months staring at the walls and waiting for the terrible announcements to begin again.

Instead the soldier appeared in his dirty boots, bowing to Mama, leaving behind the yellow telegram and the awful emptiness.

"I'm sorry, Isamu. I know you miss your father."

Mama opened her right arm for him. She was holding Hana-chan with her left. He shook his head.

And then a day came, not long ago, when the air over Tokyo filled with airplanes, hundreds and hundreds of them, bombers and smaller fighters all flying over the city at the same time. He was convinced his life was over. He was almost glad.

But they didn't drop any death. Just leaflets. The Allies were celebrating the Emperor's surrender.

He reaches the port and the wind shifts, replacing the smoke with the smells of tar and rust, the metallic tang of water.

He spies a different gang of local boys, six or seven of them, dragging and shoving a heavy box, looking behind them for pursuers. He ducks behind a huge container until the sounds of their struggle fade away.

He peeks around the corner and studies the scene. The pier never seemed so large before. Each the size of a large truck, the containers are arranged in long rows. They stretch as far as he can see.

Large, pale men are working about fifty yards away, lifting and loading wooden crates. As he gets closer, he can hear them talking to each other in a language that sounds to him like spitting.

They must be Americans.

He feels a wave of revulsion. These are the men who destroyed his life. But waiting in line for the toilet yesterday, he heard two street vendors talking about the invaders.

"Joe has so much food he doesn't know what to do with it all," one said.

Isamu means to get some. If he can only figure out where they keep it.

He swallows his disgust and approaches the men, wending past piles of equipment and large carts. One yells at him and waves him away, but he smiles and keeps coming.

Suddenly, a bulging net slams onto the asphalt, barely missing him. He jumps to the side. Huge hairy arms grab him from behind and swing him to the side. A metal box slams the concrete where he was standing.

Isamu kicks as hard as he can and feels his feet hit a man's legs. His sandals fly off and he drops to the ground.

"Ow! Take it easy, kid."

Isamu looks at the box that just missed him. Is that where they store their food? How can he steal something that heavy by himself? He needs a new plan.

He picks up a sandal. The big man hands him the other one. He gestures for Isamu to move away. He points overhead at a large crane.

Isamu watches as the massive machine lifts another bulging net. The man gently shoves him away, points to the net and shoos him.

The boy backs farther down the pier, still entranced by the crane. He skirts two other work parties, the tall Americans shouting at one another as the full nets deposit gigantic crates, jeeps, and other goods on the crowded docks.

He continues to the end, where he wraps his arms around his chest against the chill and gazes out at Tokyo Bay. All the ships that arrived in the past few days, hundreds of them, fill the harbor. Isamu is amazed. Giant battleships, dozens of smaller ships, little boats zipping from one to another. So many Americans.

How can he get one to pay attention to him?

2

Joe

The young officers are in their private clubhouse, the photo lab of the *U.S.S. Chourre*, "the greyhound of the Pacific." They're enjoying another cup of mud, their third or fourth of the day. They're always wired on caffeine.

"Cold out there today," says Jeff Wade, the ship's photographer. "This'll keep ya warm."

He pours a jolt into each cup, squinting at the smoke from the cigarette in the corner of his mouth.

"Just what the doctor ordered," laughs Doc Stephens, the ship's medic. A good-natured man, he's a little older than the other two.

"I can't wait to get ashore," says Joe Bienkunski, the communications officer. "I'm ready for some solid ground under my feet."

They'd worked hard through the sweltering summer, repairing carriers in the waters off the Philippines. No shore leave for months.

They'd steamed into Tokyo Bay at midnight, maneuvering carefully, slowly through the crowded waters to their assigned anchorage. This morning they feel buoyed. They are the victors, the first wave of the Occupation. Today is the victory lap, their first foray into the enemy's capital city.

They're so full of themselves, these ninety-day wonders. College-educated, they heeded the call. They enlisted before they were drafted and completed the three-month training to earn their officer stripes. They think of each other as the "fellas."

They lean against the tub full of chemical baths, arms crossed, relaxed in their khakis.

"It's pretty bad out there," Doc says. "The firebombing pretty much fried most of the city. That's what the exec told me."

"They deserve what they got," Wade says.

"You tell 'em, New York." Joe laughs.

Wade's a Manhattanite with a snarky accent and a superior attitude, despite his short stature. He sneers at anyone who doesn't live in "the city." Joe is an upstater, a hick to Wade.

The men go on deck, avoiding bustling sailors, and survey the huge harbor full of Allied ships. They pull their heavy jackets shut against the bitter breeze.

"Quite a sight," Joe says. Tall and stocky, always carefully groomed, he's proud to be an American.

"A mighty navy," Doc agrees.

"Ya sound like that Popeye cartoon," Wade quips, putting on his sunglasses.

On the short launch ride to the dock, he points out the white sheets draped over the shore guns ringing the harbor.

"That's meant to shame the Japs," he says.

"Like their guns have been put to sleep," Joe says.

"Yeah," Wade grins. "Like ya'd put a dog to sleep."

At the pier they come upon cranes, forklifts and men moving materiel, a sizable military operation. They commandeer the jeep that Wade had ordered for the official purpose of a photo tour of the immediate area. He insists on driving.

"It's in my name," he says, patting the dashboard, putting a new cigarette in his mouth.

"Thought you were going to take some pictures," Joe says.

Wade pops the clutch and screams down the long, shaded row between the containers.

"Christ!" Doc shouts, grabbing his hat as he's pushed against the seat. It's unusual for him to curse. He usually carries himself with quiet dignity.

Wade laughs as a couple dockworkers scurry out of his way and salute him. He takes a hard right on two wheels.

"God, this is a kick!"

As he rounds another corner, he surprises a small Japanese boy, who stands transfixed in front of the onrushing vehicle.

"Get out of the way!" Doc stands up and waves his arms. "Jump!"

At the last moment, the child throws himself to the side and the jeep barely brushes him. Wade skids to a halt.

"Jesus," says Doc, sprinting to check on the child.

"What do I know about cars?" Wade mutters, taking deep breaths, trying to calm down. "Nobody drives in the city."

The boy is shivering uncontrollably. His lips are blue.

"He's all right, as far as I can tell," Doc says. "Frightened and freezing, but not hurt."

Joe kneels next to the boy, opens his jacket and pulls the boy next to his chest.

"Hi, Joe," the boy says, looking up at him.

Joe widens his eyes and points to himself.

"How'd you know my name?"

The boy turns to Doc.

"Hi, Joe."

"We all look alike to him," Doc smiles.

"You'd think it was the middle of summer, the way he's dressed," Joe says.

The boy is in mid-length trousers with thin, strap shoes exposing his toes. His shirtsleeves end just below his elbows.

"What'll we do with him?" Joe asks.

"Leave him," Wade says.

"We can't do that," Joe says. "We almost ran him over."

"For Christ's sake, he's a Jap," Wade says.

"How about we drop him home?" Doc ventures, trying to make peace.

"Let's do it on the way back," Joe says. "Let's look around first."

They pile back into the jeep. The boy rides with Joe in the back. He's stopped shivering, but he wants to stay under Joe's jacket.

Joe points to himself, then Doc, then Wade.

"Joe. Doc. Wade." He holds his hands up in question and points to the boy. "What's your name?"

"Isamu," the boy says at once.

"Just call him Sam," Wade says.

Joe gives the boy a stick of gum and puts another in his own mouth to show him what to do.

"Just chew. Don't swallow."

Joe swallows and shakes his finger no. He opens his mouth to reveal the gum is still there.

Doc takes the wheel. They drive alongside the water for a few hundred yards and cut inland on a major thoroughfare. Wade starts snapping photos.

They pass vistas of devastation. Chimneys, remains of concrete office buildings, twisted girders, burnt wood, all covered in gray, grainy dust.

"Everything's wiped out." Doc shakes his head.

People peer at them from culverts or flimsy sheds in the lee of burned-out walls. One family is camped in a large bomb crater. They're dressed in dusty kimonos, tattered Japanese army uniforms, or bundles of rags. They skitter across the broken landscape like flies on carrion. Women stand by a faucet, drawing water. An old man drops his pants and craps.

Horse-drawn carts, rickshaws, charcoal-burning cars, and old buses crowd the streets, competing with military trucks and jeeps. People walk on the shoulders, avoiding the broken sidewalks. Soldiers stand in sentry posts on the corners.

A woman on the roadway turns to the jeep and holds out her hands, asking for help. A little farther, a second woman offers her infant to the Navy men.

They pass a long wall, fallen and cracked, gaps big enough to walk through. Inside are several destroyed structures.

Joe is the only one who notices the boy's reactions. Sometimes

Sam's eyes are wide and his mouth open. Other times he hides his face in the young officer's coat.

To Joe, Tokyo is like Mars. He's used to the sooty streets of downtown Schenectady. His world there was one square mile with the Polish ghetto at the center. No English was spoken at home. Gospels and sermons were delivered in Polish at the church on the corner. His people were poor, but proud and clean. Their lives were ordinary, but ordered.

In Tokyo, everyday existence is anything but ordered. It's shattered. The squalor is repulsive to him.

Joe draws the boy close, absently patting his back. He is so small, it's hard to guess how old he is.

They cross a double bridge and enter an area that is entirely undamaged. Carefully cultured evergreens and groves of bamboo are arranged artfully across the beautiful grounds.

"Will ya look at that," Wade quips, snapping some pictures, another cigarette dangling from his mouth.

"The Imperial Palace Grounds," Doc says.

They traverse sections of expensive homes, the slanting roofs and graceful jutting eaves untouched by the blazes, the wooden fences intact.

"How did our bombers miss these places?" Joe wonders.

"Not how," Wade mutters, taking a deep drag. "Why?"

"This is where MacArthur and the brass will live," Doc says.

They come to an area of unharmed offices in what used to be the financial district.

"Little America," Doc says. "GHQ."

The men check in at the military command before heading back. As they near the port, Joe signs for the boy to show them where he lives. Sam points across the river and the jeep detours over the Sumida.

The stench is unthinkable. Unidentifiable clumps bob in the putrid waters.

"Thank God for the cold," Doc says. "In the heat of summer,

it'd be … peh." He blows out his lips.

They move into a residential area and pull up behind a man in an ox cart piled high with household belongings. It's slow going.

"An ox!" Wade smirks, standing on the front seat to get a photo. "Can ya believe this? What a backward country."

The men creep past women and babies lurking under a few boards, past children with horrible burns.

"We'll be here all night at this rate," Doc says.

"Drop him off," Wade says. "He can find his own way home."

"Just a little farther," Joe says.

But the ox cart veers to avoid a cluster of rubbish and gets stuck in ruts of frozen mud, blocking the way.

"End of the road," Doc says.

As the jeep rolls to a stop, Sam shouts something in Japanese and points down the street. Two older boys are wrestling a sack of food away from an elderly woman.

"Hey!" Doc bellows.

"Calm down," Joe tells Sam. "There's nothing you can do."

"Fucking savages," declares Wade.

He decides he wants a photograph of their first outing, the three of them and the boy. He hands a camera to the cart driver, who is standing on the shoulder and trying to figure out what to do. Wade signs that he wants him to snap a shot.

"This will never happen," he says. "He'll never figure it out."

But the driver takes the camera reverently, backs up and frames the four subjects with great care. He gestures for Wade in his belted jacket, Doc in the back and Joe to form a semicircle around the boy.

Sam is barely half the men's height. His thin shirt seems too small, his feet so naked.

The men are wearing hats and gloves. Doc and Wade button their Navy-issue jackets and turn up their collars. Joe is used to cold weather. He leaves his jacket open and his hands bare.

They're standing in front of a leafless tree, squinting into the wintry sun. Ruins surround them.

The man with the camera grins widely and gesticulates to the men. Sam looks back up at them. They're all smiling. He smiles too.

3

Isamu

He's heard the talk around the neighborhood, boys swanking behind four-foot walls, women whispering in the open air stalls. He knows how he's supposed to think.

They're the enemy, the *gaijin*, the occupying forces. They are arrogant, ill-mannered monsters. They did monstrous things here and in Nagasaki and Hiroshima. They made war against women and children and the old.

They must be tolerated, but only until the Emperor launches his secret plan to regain the homeland and expel them once and for all. They should be shunned, whenever possible.

But to Isamu, forced to be practical, the Americans are the best shot he's got at keeping his family alive. So the next time the young officers land at the pier, there he is.

"Hi, Joe."

"Well, look who's here," Joe smiles. "Hi, Sam."

"What a surprise," Wade snickers, exhaling a cloud of smoke.

The men are looser and louder than they were before.

The last time the boy met them he had his first ride in an automobile and his first gum. He was as hungry as ever in half an hour. Now he's looking for something more filling. He wants a little for Mama too.

He falls in next to them as they walk to the motor pool. He's seen people at the marketplace make the universal sign for money, rubbing thumb and fingers together. He signs it to the officers, then points to his mouth.

"Money. Mouth," Wade interprets. "He wants ya to put money in his mouth."

Isamu can't understand what he's saying, but he can smell the alcohol on his breath. He isn't carrying any camera gear this time.

"He wants money to buy food," Doc says.

Joe offers another stick of gum, but Isamu refuses. He pretends to cradle a baby and points back over his shoulder toward home.

"A baby back home," Doc says.

"Christ, what is he? Eight, nine?" Joe says. "And he's got a family to feed?"

"He could be ten, I'd guess," Doc says. "Malnutrition, you know."

From the way the men relate to him, the tone of voice when they speak to him, Isamu suspects they think he is younger than he is. He turned twelve last spring. How can he take advantage of their error?

The boy points to himself, holds his arms wide and then waves his arm in a semicircle.

"He's saying he can show us around," Joe says.

"Let's go," Wade says, lighting another cigarette.

Isamu climbs in the back seat with Joe, like last time, but he stands behind the driver. He's dressed more warmly today, wearing a light sweater and socks, along with his too-small shirt, shorts, and sandals.

"Where to?" Doc asks.

"Somewhere to buy some hootch," Wade says.

"I could use a shoeshine," Joe says.

Joe takes a pull on an imaginary bottle, then points to the boy, then sweeps the neighborhood.

Isamu points forward. Doc drives for a couple minutes before the boy taps him on the shoulder and motions for him to wait. He makes the money sign and points partway up the street toward a stooped man with a beard shaped like a shovel. He holds out his palm.

"That's where you buy booze?" Wade asks, pointing his cigarette. He gives the boy a few coins.

Isamu scoots over to the man, bows politely, gives him a

single coin and asks a question. The man points to the northwest.

Back in the jeep, the boy taps Doc on either shoulder when he wants him to turn. All the road signs are gone.

They find a shack selling liquor in ten blocks. Isamu runs over and purchases a jar of sake. He pockets one coin and returns the rest to Wade.

The shoeshine is next. Isamu asks directions from a boy on the street and guides the men to where several women are cleaning sailors' shoes. Joe pays for all three shines. He notices when the women slip a couple coins to the boy, but he doesn't say anything.

Their shoes are soiled as soon as the men walk back to the jeep.

"See if he can find us some 'comfort women,'" Wade laughs, making a crude hand gesture.

"I think he's too young to know what that means," Joe says.

Wrong. Isamu understands Wade's sign. He's seen women behind his hotel, bending over, raising their skirts. He inquires of an old woman and then directs the men to an intact housing block, where a large sign in American letters stretches over the front: *Wellcome Joe!*

Hundreds of American sailors, wearing their whites with their Dixie cup caps, crowd eight-across in front of the building. Some are playing cards and a few are drinking, but everyone is orderly. MPs patrol the perimeter.

"A lot different than the red light district back home," Joe says.

"The Brass is turning a blind eye," Doc says. "Lots of rapes of local women. The Japs are hoping this'll cut that down."

Women with babies shelter in the shadows across the street. There are no other girls in sight.

"Wonder if there's a special line for officers?" Wade asks.

While the men are talking, Isamu reaches for the side compartment on the driver's door and pulls out a comb, a pencil and the real prize, a pack of cigarettes. He puts the comb and pencil back and sneaks the cigarettes into his pants.

Joe sees the theft, but he looks away when Isamu glances over at him.

"I don't think we should be seen standing in that line," Doc says.

"Besides, it would take forever," Joe says.

"Shit!" Wade says, smashing his bottle on the street.

"C'mon, Lieutenant," Doc says.

Wade turns to the boy. "Is that the best ya can do?"

Isamu ducks his head and falls back into the seat. He gets a bad feeling from Wade. He doesn't like the way the shorter man with the cigarettes looks at him.

"It's not his fault," Joe says.

Isamu rubs his stomach and whines.

Joe responds by pulling a sandwich out of an inside pocket of his jacket. He tears it in two and gives half to the boy.

Isamu wolfs the food, then looks up at the officer. He tries to smile sweetly like a little boy.

This American seems to notice more than the other two. They already stopped registering the wreckage and decay, but not this one. He still stares across the desolate streets like it's the first time he's seen them. He's the softest target. And the boy knows that he's always watching him.

Joe isn't his friend, but Isamu isn't afraid of him. Not all monsters are alike.

* * *

On the next trip two days later, Isamu knows in advance where the men want to go, so he is able to get detailed directions before he meets them.

They drive for nearly an hour before Isamu holds up his hand to stop. He points behind a building, where sunlight glints off something greenish and metallic.

It's the Great Buddha of Kamakura, sitting in lotus position, a massive statue seven times the size of a man. Isamu joins hands and bows to the massive bronze.

"Buddha," he says.

"Da Budda," says Wade, who has been drinking steadily during the entire trip. "Da Budda had a brudda ..."

"Who coulda been big," Doc chimes in, chuckling.

And Wade comes back: "But da Budda was a pig and wouldn't share."

He roars with delight at his own wet wit, holding his hands in front of an imaginary fat belly. The few Japanese in the area glance at him with irritation, but quickly look away.

"Is there a place to take a piss around here?" Wade wonders. He pantomimes unzipping his fly and holding his cock.

Isamu backs away, shaking his head, and bumps into Joe, nearly knocking him down.

"Jesus, Wade," Joe says.

Wade shoots the finger at him and walks behind the statue to relieve himself.

Eyes wide, horrified, the boy scuttles away and waits for the officers by the jeep.

When they get back to the port, Joe puts his arm around Isamu's shoulder and takes a few steps to the side. He reaches into his jacket pocket, removes a paper bag and sneaks it under the boy's shirt.

"At least it's something."

Isamu looks under his shirt and sees the sandwich. He looks up and nods.

"Domo," he says.

Hugging himself tightly, he runs away as fast as he can.

4

Joe

The men are thousands of miles from home, often hundreds from landfall, frequently lost in fog and waves. They have no way of knowing what's happening in the war or what they're supposed to do, sometimes even where they are, unless the communications officer tells them.

That's Joe.

The information arrives at Radio Central, where enlisted men work in spaces so crowded with electronic equipment that they have to squeeze by each other sideways. Pipes clutter the ceiling. Everything is cold, gray metal.

Operators in headsets transcribe incoming dots and dashes into sequences of numbers and words. They have no idea what the numbers and words mean until they take them next door to the crypto room.

That's where Joe spends long hours by himself, painstakingly entering the sequences on a decoding machine that looks like a typewriter. Only he and the exec have clearance to decipher the messages beaming aboard *Chourre*.

During baseball season, Joe takes the time every day to decode the major league box scores, so that the sailors can follow their hometown teams and favorite players. The scores are transmitted in Morse code to all the ships at sea when there are no orders or official operational data to send.

Joe thinks it's good for morale. President Roosevelt thought the same thing when he permitted the leagues to continue their seasons during the war years.

Joe loves the statistics in baseball, the way they wrinkle and ripple and settle, the way one revision causes dozens of others. He sees the numbers as facts. They're real, reassuring, true. Kind of like orders aboard ship. Like their belief that their enemies are evil. Baseball is something they can count on.

Joe hardly played ball as a boy. He was too busy making deliveries, helping out at the neighborhood store his parents operated. He fell in love with the sport in this place where there are no groomed green fields, no chalked enclosures, only the endless waters of the Pacific Ocean.

He copies the scores for each team in his careful, legible script and takes them to Cookie, who posts them in the mess hall. As a result, Joe is popular with the seamen. When he asks Cookie to make a few extra sandwiches for him, it's no problem, doesn't give it a second thought.

Joe has a son, not quite two years old when he shipped out. He hardly knows him, but he thinks about him often. Good Catholic that he is, he's guilty about not being there to help raise him. That might have something to do with the fatherly feelings he has for the Japanese boy. That's the topic of discussion at lunch in the wardroom.

"You ain't his daddy, Joey-boy," Wade says. "Don't give him any more. He'll just keep pestering ya."

"It's just a few sandwiches," Joe says. "It can't do any harm."

"Next thing ya know, you come ashore and thousands of little Nips will follow you, demanding food for their families."

"He's hungry," Joe says.

"They all are, every one of them," Doc says. "That's why MacArthur is shipping in food."

"That's what they get for killing Americans," Wade says. "They're getting off easy, in my opinion."

"We ought to do more," Joe says.

"I think Binky's running for office," Wade says. "Governor of Nipland. He wants to feed the masses."

"Ha!" Doc chuckles in his good-natured way, "Binky's legions."

"We ought to give 'em the food we throw away," Joe insists.

"Are ya crazy?" Wade demands. "We won't be able to go anywhere. They'll be on our backs the whole time. Ya heard what the exec said."

The executive officer told the men to stay away from the locals.

"Don't trust 'em," he said. "They'll glom onto anything you own and sell it on the black market. Even the kids'll do it."

"Japs are vermin," Wade says. "They're dirty." He grimaces and brushes imaginary dirt off his sleeve. "They've got no right to our grub."

Make no mistake, Joe is a naval officer, fiercely proud to be a member of the club. But he's sensitive to slurs, abuse, abasements. He's a Polack, the second son of an illegal immigrant. Throughout his school years, all the way through college, he was the target of bullies and the butt of endless jibes about his nationality.

During the Depression, he saw his folks feed their neighbors, selling groceries to them on credit. Much of it was never repaid. They did it because they had to. That's how his father explained it. Not could. Not should. Had to.

"I just don't think they should starve," Joe says.

Wade rolls his eyes. Doc shakes his head and smiles.

The three young officers agree on another excursion, this time to the underground tunnels at Matsushiro. Sam, of course, is their tour guide.

Joe brings a sack with two sandwiches stuffed in his jacket. He pats his jacket so the boy knows he has something to give him after the trip.

They putter south past vast landscapes of wreckage, dodging huge potholes, beeping at children standing in the middle of dirt streets.

In one neighborhood where a few wooden structures are still standing, dozens of smiling children clamber onto the jeep. Sam ducks behind the front seat and grabs onto Joe's leg, trying to secure his place.

The men empty their pockets, shoveling gum, candies, even cigarettes into the hungry swarm.

"Have you ever seen anything like that?" Doc asks.

At Matsushiro, they stroll the huge caverns, where the Japanese government planned to build factories, docks for their ships, even a scaled-down version of the Imperial shrine. They were 75 percent completed when work stopped.

The men are astounded at the immensity, stretching under several mountains. They're amazed at the human cost of construction, which is described in hand-lettered signs pasted around the complex. Thousands died, many of them Korean prisoners.

Doc points to a brand-new Mercedes parked against one wall. "That's the old man's."

The captain saw the car on a prior tour and claimed it for himself. It's scheduled to be loaded aboard before the ship departs.

The caves are littered with construction gear, military equipment, uniforms, and other clothing. The workers apparently dropped everything and left the job when the Emperor surrendered.

Joe discovers a small room plastered with posters of Japanese baseball players. In one corner are canvas bags full of bats, balls, gloves, catchers' chest and shin protectors, bases, and uniforms.

"I didn't even know they played baseball," he says.

"We helped them get it going before the war," Wade says. "Some Americans played over here."

Wade is a big baseball fan. With three teams in New York, it's hard not to be.

Sam stares at the posters of famous players, but shows no interest in the equipment. The men pack a canvas sack full of gear for themselves.

When he hands over Cookie's lunch at the end of the day, Joe points to the bag, then points away, then points to the boy. He holds his hands wide with a questioning expression of his face. Where do you go?

Sam pantomimes sleeping, the place where he sleeps, home.

Joe makes the fingers of one hand run over the back of his other hand, then raises his eyebrows. Why did you run?

The boy makes grabbing motions with both hands and looks around fearfully. He's afraid someone will take his food.

Joe scowls and grips Sam's shoulder reassuringly. His father used to do that to him. He takes off his cap, turns it over and packs the sandwiches inside. He hands it to the boy.

Sam puts the hat on his head carefully and gently pushes it down. It's much too large, but the food keeps it above his ears. He has to smile.

Joe too.

5

Isamu

He dumps the night soil into the ditch everyone has been using. The stink follows him across the block back to their room. He hopes the rains will bring relief from the reek soon.

Later he will help Mama gather provisions, but this morning he makes his way to the river and over the bridge to the docks. He takes his time. No sense getting there too early. Joe never appears before 10:00 a.m.

He's developed alternate routes across the ravaged lots, taking advantage of standing buildings, windbreaks, hidey holes, and little-used paths. Isamu stays alert for bigger boys, for people he knows or for opportunities.

He'd found a smelly blanket the day before. He had no way to launder it, but he managed to trade it for a scarf, which he tried to give to Mama. She insisted he wear it.

He wraps it around his neck and his mouth and plunks his oversized Navy hat on his head. He disappears into his clothing.

The landscape is constantly evolving, piles of debris disappearing, sections of buildings being exposed. People relocate to better shelters. Black marketeers set up stalls and tear them down in a few days.

How much easier it would be if Riku were with him, Isamu thinks. The two used to be inseparable. His friend was a jokester. He could find a way to make anything fun, even scraping by day-to-day. He would have made a game of it.

Like most children, Riku left Tokyo and went to the countryside to live with his relatives when food shortages and power outages got worse. Mama has no family outside the city, so they had no place to go.

Isamu watches as Joe moves closer across the choppy bay.

While the pilot idles the small craft at the pier, the young officer hops out and hands the boy a bulging sack.

"Three days' worth," he says, holding up three fingers.

He pats Isamu on the cap and chuckles.

The boy takes four sandwiches out of the bag and inserts them in his hat, which he puts back on his head. It rides considerably higher.

Joe laughs again. He laughs a lot. Isamu likes that.

"I'd like to meet your parents," Joe says. "I'd like to figure out a way to help them."

The boy doesn't understand.

Joe signs. Sleeping, you, me, away. Take me to your home.

Isamu gets it, but he shrugs as if he doesn't. He doesn't want to refuse the man. That could cut off the supply of food. He bows to him and trots back the way he came.

He thinks of the lectures they used to endure at school. Each morning a soldier brought a sheet of paper to the teacher, who made the students stand before he read it to the class. The papers were about the Americans, their adversaries, how they were soulless demons. Every day there were new examples. The Americans enslave their citizens. They're sadistic. They're unclean.

Twice each month, the children sat quietly in the lunchroom and listened to a man with a chest shining with medals. He told them the Americans are evil and they only care about themselves.

Then why is Joe feeding him?

The boy prefers the coins that the men give him after a tour. American money goes a long way in the stalls. But the men haven't gone anywhere in the last week and Isamu doesn't have the nerve to rub his fingers together to Joe. He doesn't want to push his luck.

Why does Joe want to come to his home?

Back at the room, Mama puts the sandwiches on a plate. She is almost ready for their neighborhood expedition. She had changed from her baggy, worn pantaloons and tattered blouse to a plain brown kimono, the best outfit she has left. She carefully arranges a comb in her hair. She straps the baby to her back, using twine and a burlap sack. She brings a second sack and she hands Isamu a pail.

On the way down the stairs, she takes the hat off his head.

"American," she says. "Shame, shame."

"It's mine," her son says, reaching for it. "Give it back."

"I am your mother." She slaps his hand. "Don't be rude. Don't call attention."

She puts the hat in her sack.

"It keeps me warm. You might as well take this too."

He unwinds his scarf and tosses it at Mama. It falls at her feet.

She keeps her back straight so she won't disturb the infant as she lowers and picks it up. She stashes the scarf in the sack.

"Americans. Pah! They teach you to be this way."

Mama pulls her son close as they step outdoors. She peers around furtively. It seems to the boy that she becomes an old woman.

She always loved to shop. Isamu remembers going with her, reaching up to hold her hand, as they strolled all the way to the train station. She was so elegant, so beautiful. Everyone admired her. Sales clerks jostled to serve her, she had such exquisite taste. An officer's wife, she had leisure to appreciate their offerings and she was generous with her compliments.

Now she doesn't want to chat. She doesn't want to meet anybody's eyes. She's like all the rest of them. She's meek and quick. She doesn't want to be here any longer than she must.

Isamu is worried about her. She is thin and wan. The baby doesn't let her sleep. Yet she is stronger from the food he brings home. She has milk again. She has more energy than when they only ate the thin rice gruel. They both do.

Everything is in short supply. The most ordinary household items are scarce since the fires. The cost of fresh produce, when you can find it, is outrageous. Salted fish, miso, they haven't been available for weeks.

Mama spent the last of the coins Isamu brought home a week ago. She barters with a woman in a stall she's never seen before. She trades some shirts her son has outgrown. She had hoped to save them for the baby. She finds some sweet potatoes and some wheat bran. There is no rice.

A young girl with a swollen belly sucks on an orange peel. Two small boys struggle with arms full of scrap wood. On another woman's back, a skinny baby cries feebly and lolls his head.

Mama lines up at the neighborhood faucet. She keeps turning her head to see in all directions. Young hooligans come sometimes and steal the women's groceries.

Isamu fills the pail with drinking water and strains to carry it. He spills some of it climbing the stairs.

Mama is tired when they get back. The baby is squalling. She still wants to talk.

"I ... I thank you for what you're doing. It's important to our family. Your sister thanks you too."

She turns away as she takes out her breast. She looks over her shoulder.

"Your father would be proud of you. I am proud."

"Thank you, Mama."

Isamu looks down, roiling with conflicting feelings.

His father would never have thanked him. The man was imperious. Everyone was expected to obey him, not just the servants in their fine officer's quarters. Everyone, especially his only son. He never earned his father's affection, only his disapproval.

"You, boy, make yourself straight." Isamu remembered the constant admonition, his father's hand in the middle of his back. "Let people see you are proud."

He never minded when his father went away on extended

assignments. He didn't miss him then. But now with all their privilege gone, with everyday existence so difficult, it was impossible not to remember how easy it had been.

"I wish you didn't feel like you have to do this," Mama says.

"I want to do it, Mama. I can't just sit here. Not anymore."

She turns back to her nursing infant, wipes her face and fusses.

"I'm glad that you're going out," she says so softly he has to strain to hear, "but I am ... troubled about the Americans."

"Ha! That's when I'm safest."

"That may be. It may not," she says, glancing over her shoulder, scowling at his outburst. "But how far you must travel to get to these men."

"I can take care of myself. You worry too much."

"Don't be disrespectful. You sound like an American."

"I'm a man now," he insists.

She shakes her head.

"Almost."

She lays Hana-*chan* on her shoulder and turns back to her son.

"This man who gave you those ... those meat things," she says, trying to sound sure of herself. "I would like to talk to him. But I can't carry Hana-*chan* all that way. Would he come here?"

Isamu is taken aback. He hasn't told her about Joe's request. He assumed she'd refuse.

He thinks of Joe pointing at himself and pointing across the blocks. He hears his laugh. Maybe it isn't such a bad idea. Then she wouldn't worry so much. And Joe might feel obligated.

"He might. I will ask."

She holds up two fingers. "I will serve tea in two days."

"How can we pay for tea?"

Mama reaches into the burlap, grinning, and holds up Joe's hat.

6

Joe

"What are you doing, Joe?" Doc asks in his mild way when Cookie brings in another sack of sandwiches. "You can't take care of that kid. You're not going to be around."

"When are we shipping out?" Joe wants to know.

"Nothing definite, but I'm told I should finish getting my medical supplies together as soon as I can."

"Right after Christmas is what I hear," says Wade, rubbing his palms together.

The "fellas" are sharing a cup of coffee in the wardroom after coming off the morning watch. They're talking about Sam again.

"You're just setting him up for a fall," Doc says.

"I don't know. I just can't turn my back on him."

"They made it on their own before we arrived," Doc says. "They'll do it themselves after we've left."

"He's a survivor," Wade says, "filthy little fucker."

Joe scowls at him.

"What?" Wade says. "Ya seen his feet?"

When Joe meets him at the pier an hour later, Sam is bareheaded. Several other local boys, all larger, are also waiting for "their" Americans.

"Where'd it go?" Joe asks, pointing to his head and shrugging.

Sam doesn't answer. He turns and trots away. He pauses after a few paces and looks back with an impatient expression. Are you coming?

"Why don't we walk together?" Joe mutters to himself, putting the full sack under his arm and following the boy. Why did he invite me if he doesn't want to be seen with me?

They traverse the ruins in single file. The boy slows to a fast walk and rarely looks back. Joe has to hurry to keep up.

He's interested to see where the boy lives. A corner lean-to, covered in cardboard or scraps of wood, like the ones he sees next to the dirt road? Family members crunched and shriveled like the people huddling in alleyways?

The filth is hard to believe. The dullness in people's eyes. Joe shivers and pulls his jacket tight around his neck. The chill seems to touch the bone.

Sam leads him to an old hotel, tilted slightly to one side, nearly a mile from the docks. They climb narrow steps. Open doors reveal dingy rooms, people who don't bother to look up. Joe brings his hand to his nose to block the odor. On the third floor, at the head of the stairs, the boy opens a grayish door.

She waits in a pale pool of light, a sleeping baby in her arms. She is tiny, excruciatingly feminine.

Joe thought he'd encounter someone smudged and slovenly, like he's seen on the streets. But this woman is neat and trim, immaculate.

He inclines his head. He takes off his hat, puts it in his back pocket and steps inside.

The room is small, about fifteen feet across. It's neat and bare – tattered straw mats on the floor, a few bruised cushions, a couple of low tables containing photos, etc., a small charcoal burner, a kitchen area. The walls are empty, although there are several pallid rectangles where pictures or coverings used to hang. Sam is putting his shoes on a strip of concrete by the entrance. Joe hardly sees him.

He points to himself.

"Joe. Joe Bienkunski." He holds out his hand.

She hesitates, touching her throat, and then enunciates, "Aiko," and looks down.

"Eye-ko," Joe repeats softly. He lowers his hand.

Sam takes the infant, says—"Hana-*chan*"—and moves to a far corner.

Apparently just the three of them. No man of the house. No

signs of one.

"*Yokoso*," the woman says, her eyes straying to the sack in Joe's hand.

He has no idea what she's talking about. Is she asking what he's carrying?

Sam points to her and opens his hands wide. She is welcoming him.

Joe nods. He hands her the bag.

"*Arigato*," she says and bows.

When she sees that he doesn't understand, she gestures to the bag, and smiles before dropping her eyes.

She's completely different from the woman waiting back home. Joe's wife is long and rangy, her manner direct. She moved back into her mother's house for the duration. He thinks of the uncomfortable overstuffed chairs, the heavy mahogany of the dining room table.

The woman sets the bag down. She picks up a cup, which she offers to Joe, at the same time motioning him to a cushion.

"*O-cha?*"

"*O-cha?*" Joe repeats.

He sits awkwardly, unsure where to put his feet. He brings his knees up, smiling at her as she pours steaming liquid into his cup. It's some sort of Jap brew, probably tea. He hates tea. It's something you drink when you're sick, when you have a fever.

She retrieves a second mismatched cup, then pulls up another cushion and sits, her legs together to the side.

She holds the cup high and smiles at Joe. She looks down shyly, but he can tell that she's appraising him. She's wearing a brown kimono with a white sash across her middle. Her hair is below her ears and she's combed it across her head, almost like a man.

She sips. Joe gulps and tries to keep a pleasant expression in his face, despite the bitter taste. He longs for sugar.

Joe is thirty years old. He has been at sea since spring. He hasn't seen his young wife since his four-day leave ten months ago.

He studies the woman. She looks down demurely. She's a young woman of … what … 25 or so? Her features are miniatures. She smells like some sort of flower, he can't place what.

Aiko rises, gets the teapot, and refills his cup.

As she sits again, Joe points to himself and then opens his hands to include the entire room. Me. Here, this place.

He pauses to think, then signs a circular motion from chest and offers opened hands again. Give.

The woman nods. Yes. She puts her hands together and bows.

She thinks he is thanking her. How can he signify what he means? He opens his hands again to indicate the room. Then he puts one hand on his chest and stretches the other hand toward the room. A questioning shrug. What can I do?

Aiko is puzzled.

"I feel like I'm playing a child's game," Joe laughs.

Sam laughs with him, which startles Joe. He's almost forgotten the boy is in the room.

The infant starts spitting and grunting. There is an unmistakable aroma. Sam works with the baby's clothing. A trace of humor flickers at the corner of the woman's mouth and immediately disappears.

Joe points to himself. To her. To the boy and infant. Makes the circular motion and shrugs. How can I help you? Them?

The woman smiles softly. She seems to do everything that way. He doesn't think she understands.

He takes another swig of the wretched tea, sweeps his eyes around the blank walls, the barren room. The window looks out on the wooden wall of a neighboring building.

He's a little unmoored. He hears Doc in his head: "What are you doing, Joe?"

He laughs again, a little self-consciously. The woman and the boy laugh too.

These people are destitute. He should have surmised as much by the fact that the boy is begging, but he never thought about it. What an impossible situation. They need ... everything.

Curiosity, that's what really brought him here. He wondered where the boy was from. He shouldn't have come.

Apparently, Aiko is curious too. She points to the bag of food and raises her shoulders in a shrug. Why did you bring food?

Joe points to the boy and rubs his stomach. I saw he was hungry.

Sam stuffs the soiled diaper in a pail in the corner of the room and covers it with a plate. The odor starts to dissipate.

Aiko points to her son and shrugs. Why him?

Joe points to Sam and flexes his bicep. "Strong."

Sam grins, as he sits again, holding his sister on his shoulder. The woman is watchful.

Joe points to Sam and taps his head. "Smart."

Aiko nods.

Joe points to the boy and then to himself. He sweeps one arm in a wide semicircle, then the other arm in the same way. He shows me all around.

She sits back and glances at her son.

Something has been decided. Joe can feel it. He has passed some test and then he, himself a parent, gets it. She wanted to know why he was involved with her son. She wanted to make sure his intentions were honorable.

He points to the boy, nods, and smiles. She returns his smile.

There's nothing more to say. Joe would like to sit and stare at her for a while, a long while, but he knows he can't do that. He looks at his watch. He stands and holds out his half-full cup.

Aiko stands and takes the cup. She murmurs something he can't understand. Thank you? I hope I see you again? She bows again to the American.

"Joe-*san*," she says softly.

A pang of ... what? He doesn't know. He ignores it. God,

she's lovely.

"I … I am pleased to meet you," he says. "Thank you for inviting me into your home."

He puts his hat under his arm and clicks his Navy regulation heels together, scrunching up the mat.

He bows to the woman and nods to the boy. He executes a brisk about-face on the slippery straw and departs, the sharp slap of his steps fading as he descends the stairs.

7

Isamu

Mama hands Isamu a meat thing from the bag Joe left and takes a polite bite of her own, grimacing at the taste.

"I guess Hana-*chan* drove him out," he says.

"He was no match for her," Mama says.

They share quiet smiles, amused by the American's abrupt exit.

"Do you have any idea what he said before he left?" Mama asks.

"He kept repeating the same motions," Isamu says, waving his arms to mimic the American's gestures. "He seemed to want something."

"What could we have that he needs?"

"Something else to drink? I don't think he liked the tea."

Mama laughs out loud.

She changes into her blouse and pantaloons, wets a rag and gets down on her hands and knees to clean the mat where Joe walked without removing his shoes.

"He's different than I expected," she says, scrubbing a muddy stain, "but I think you will be okay with this man. He has nice eyes."

Isamu is relieved that she feels better about Joe. He's not sure of his own feelings. The young naval officer fascinates him. He likes his uniform, the way he holds himself, his officer's bearing. He fills a room.

Like Father did.

The American is larger and stockier than Father, and, with his wide eyes and his moon face, he's "monster" ugly. Yet he's different than the other officers. He seems to be more affected by what he sees around the city. He seems to care more than the others do.

Is he the enemy?

He resents that the Americans are in his country. He blames them for the terrible conditions in Tokyo and he fears what else they will do. But he is thankful for the food and he's comfortable with Joe, his easy manner and personal warmth.

Isamu continues his regular excursions. It's getting colder. He can see his breath most mornings. He's glad Mama gave him back his scarf.

He makes a deal with the owner of a charcoal shop to get coals in exchange for scrap lumber he scavenges on the scorched lots. He manages to recover enough to keep the ice off the inside of the room window.

It's hard, dirty work that often takes him inside abandoned buildings. He comes upon several frozen corpses, all of their clothing removed. In one unoccupied shelter, he finds a dead man still wearing shoes.

It's too bitter to go barefoot any longer. They almost fit. Close enough to wear.

He searches all the way to the shipyards. When he sees Joe every day or so, he stashes the sandwiches under the scrap wood. Without the cap, he has nowhere else to hide them.

"Say hi to Aiko," Joe says the first time he meets him after his visit to their home. He lifts an imaginary cup and grins. He gives Isamu some chocolates.

Two days later, he hands the boy nylons, clearly not for him. Another time, British tea. That brings a smile from the boy. He and Mama use the gifts for barter, except for the candies. Those they eat greedily.

One afternoon, Joe gives him a double set of U.S. Navy dishes, including cups, plates, bowls, knives, forks, and spoons. Including the food and wood, it makes quite a load.

He's usually careful to vary his route to be purposely unpredictable, but he gets careless with his heavy load. He takes the shortest way home.

It's particularly gloomy. He can hardly see the sun. He can barely feel his hands. Isamu hurries to get out of the chill. He steadies his load with his chin.

Suddenly shoved from behind, he sprawls on his face, his treasures tumbling into the ash and dust. Three bigger boys surround him, laughing loudly.

"Look what we have here!" Kiro, a chubby kid shouts. "Lunch for everyone."

He kicks Isamu.

"Thanks for bringing it to us, stupid boy." Ato, a boy with a terrible burn on one side of his face, reaches down and cuffs Isamu on the ear.

The third one, Takeo, yanks Isamu to his feet and shouts at him.

"Where did you get this stuff? This is *gaijin* food."

"Leave me alone! Let me be!"

The boy throws Isamu to the ground again. He curls into a fetal ball as all three kick him, stuffing their mouths with sandwiches at the same time.

"*Kuso!* Who do you think you are?"

"Stay away from here! This is our territory!"

They pick up the wood, the food, and the ceramic dishes and walk away, leaving Isamu like spoiled fruit in the dirt. He crawls behind a discarded refrigerator and loses consciousness.

He wakes hours later, teeth chattering in a cold wind. His ribs hurt whenever he moves. So does his head. His knee is scraped and twisted. There are cuts on his face, one eye is swollen shut, and a front tooth is missing.

He manages to limp home, arriving just before dark. He's wheezing and he can't get warm.

Aiko is horrified. She cleans and tends his wounds, weeping softly.

Isamu sleeps for two days, wakes, and slurps a bowl of rice

gruel and sleeps for another twenty-four hours.

He groans and sits up, wraps his arms around himself gingerly. Mama puts a shawl around his shoulders and brings him a glass of water. Isamu drinks deeply.

She serves another cup of gruel and he looks at her with his one open eye.

"Is this all we've got, Mama?"

"I haven't been able to shop. I had to watch over you."

He gulps the soup and puts the cup down.

"This isn't enough."

"It will do for today."

Isamu coughs.

"Tomorrow morning," he says.

"You're not going back there," Mama says. "I told you it was too dangerous."

"How do we eat then? What do we do for food?"

The boy seems to have aged overnight. He sighs like an old man.

"What, Mama? Trade our stove? Our sleeping mats? My sister?"

Aiko gasps. Isamu laughs.

"Don't worry. She's too young, even for the Americans."

"Dreadful boy, where do you learn such things?"

8

Joe

It's the day after Thanksgiving. Joe is still stuffed from Cookie's feast. He sits at the crypto machine, listening to the electronic belches, decoding the daily messages. He's cranky, claustrophobic amid the pulsing and humming technology.

He hasn't seen Sam for a week. Where is he? Every day Joe grabs some sandwiches and takes the launch to shore, but there's no one there to meet him. What's going on? Is the boy all right?

Did he do something to offend him or his mother?

He wants to see her again.

Not much was accomplished by his visit to Sam's room. He wasn't able to communicate with her. She didn't really grasp what he was asking her. If he wants to help them, he'll have to figure it out on his own.

At least he's found where they live. They aren't squatting in some lean-to like so many others. But he could tell times are tough for them. It looked like they'd sold everything down to the bare walls. Do they have enough to eat? He wishes he'd been more observant, but he couldn't take his eyes off her.

He wants to see her again.

He can't get her out of his mind. Tiny Aiko. Why is he in such turmoil? He's alarmed at the intensity of his feelings, angry at himself, but he can't stop them.

How brave she is, raising two kids on her own in such devastation. But she acted like there was nothing out of the ordinary. Two parents talking over tea. She concealed any personal distress and treated him with respect. He admires her.

More than that, he desires her.

He tries to be logical. It makes no sense to get involved with a Japanese woman. Orders have come in and he'll be departing in about six weeks. *Chourre* is sailing on January 7. They'll be stateside by early May.

Plus he's married. He tamps down a glint of guilt. He hasn't done anything. All he's doing is ... what? ... imagining?

There's no reason to think that she's interested in him. She was the image of propriety, looking down, preparing tea to thank him for the food. That's all. There was no suggestion of anything else.

Was there?

He hears her soft voice again: "Joe-*san*."

It's just him. He's randy as a goat. He hasn't been with a woman for too long. He should take Wade up on his offer to go to the comfort stations.

But there's something else. He feels a link with Aiko, a leaning, a yearning he hopes might be shared.

He knows he can't let the "fellas" know about it. They'd never let him live it down. They'd never shut up about it.

He rides the launch to shore, even though he doesn't see anyone waiting for him. He's got the usual bag of sandwiches. He's decided he'll leave it on the dock on the chance that the boy might get it later. If someone else finds it instead, so what.

The seaman pops the engine into reverse as he docks and Joe watches the prop agitating the water. It looks like how his gut feels.

As he reaches the pier, he makes out a small shape in the distance, moving slowly. Joe waits for what seems like a long time while the figure comes toward him between the rows of containers. It's Sam.

"Where have you been?" Joe sounds angry, but he's actually relieved. "I brought sandwiches a bunch of times, but you weren't here."

Then he notices his black eye and the cuts and bruises all over the boy's face.

"What happened to you?"

Sam holds both hands up – big. He puts his hands around his neck. He punches the air. He covers his head and snuffles, starts crying.

Joe is furious.

"*Psiakrew!*" he says, reverting to Polish. Damn it!

The boy thinks Joe is angry with him. He backs up two steps, three, and then collapses in tears.

Joe kneels and puts his arm around him. He pats his back awkwardly with the hand clutching the sandwiches, and then stands back.

"Tell me what happened."

Still sobbing, Sam looks down and doesn't respond. He doesn't understand.

"Where?" Joe waves his arm. "Was your mother there? Aiko?"

The boy looks up at the name, shakes his head.

Relieved, Joe mimes yanking something away from the boy. "What did they take?"

The boy pretends to drink from a cup, to eat from a plate.

"I wish I knew how to protect you," Joe mutters, folding the boy back into his jacket.

That night as he paces the deck on watch, Joe keeps reliving the scene with the boy. How maddening it must be for Sam. How difficult for Aiko. There must be something he can do.

The grocer's son comes up with a typical American solution. Maybe he can provide enough food so people won't need to steal from them, at least in the short term. While he's at it, maybe he can confer a sort of status on Sam and his mother that can serve to shield them.

The next day Joe stops by the galley, where Cookie is peeling potatoes.

"Something the matter, Lieutenant?"

Joe shakes his head.

"Why do you ask?"

"Don't mind me sayin', sir, but you look pooped. Been pullin' extra duty?"

"Not sleeping great, that's all," Joe says. "It's depressing out there."

"Not where I been goin'."

Cookie surrenders to wheezy, jiggly whooping. He's not a slender man.

Joe laughs tiredly, as the man hands him a couple sandwiches.

"Say, Cookie, what do you do with the leftover food around here?"

"Toss it overboard, most of it. Feed the fishes."

"How much of it is there?"

"Not a lot. Usually a couple pails."

"Why not give it to the Japs?"

"Rather not, sir."

"Why not? We're just throwing it away."

"Lost a lot of friends, sir."

Joe nods. "Half the men in my OCS class. It's been a long, ugly war."

"That it has, sir."

"But the people out there," Joe gestures toward shore, "the women and children, they didn't kill anybody."

Cookie looks down.

"If I asked you to save tonight's leftovers for me, would you refuse me?"

"No sir. Never do that, sir. Not if you want it."

"I appreciate it, Cookie. I'll pick it up early tomorrow."

Over a later supper, he asks Doc to help with the delivery.

"You're not thinking this out, Joe," Doc tells him. "These people, they'll never get enough."

"They're not like that," Joe says. "They are good, modest people."

"What are they going to do when you're gone?"

"I've got to do something. I can't do nothing."

It's not a new dispute between them. Doc gives in because he knows that, if he doesn't, Joe will try to do it by himself.

Next morning there is more grub than Joe counted on, four big pails full. He needs a cart to carry them. Doc convinces Joe to cover the pails with a tarp so the food isn't visible.

"Don't ask for trouble," he says.

They wrestle the pails and cart aboard the launch and offload them on shore. They're sweating with the effort, despite the chill.

It's a twenty-minute walk to Sam's room, if you aren't pushing a heavy cart over muddy streets. Halfway there, a wheel comes off the cart. The men try to fix it, but they need a few tools. Doc trots back to the ship, while Joe waits with the load.

A breeze blows off the water that cuts through Joe's jacket. It lifts swirls of dust and ash across the crushed landscape. It disperses the odors of the food.

The pails are full of beef stew, one of Cookie's all-purpose meals that include every food group. They're tilting, ever so slightly, because the front wheel is askew.

Joe walks slowly around the cart, trying to be offhand and official at the same time. The street is mostly empty, though a few people go by, holding their wraps closed at their necks.

Joe flaps his arms across his chest to stay warm, a piece of luck.

That sound stops the first dog long enough for Joe to notice him. The mutt, a smallish spaniel mix, lowers himself into the rubble, ears perked.

A second dog comes around a corner of a building. A third appears, arriving like the others from downwind.

Joe didn't think there were any dogs left in Tokyo. He'd heard that people ate them. Apparently not all of them.

Joe glances behind him. There are no dogs, but a couple children are standing in the street and watching.

"Go away," he motions with his arm. "Get out of here before you get hurt."

He picks up some clots of dirt and advances on the animals.

Joe isn't afraid of dogs. The streets of Schenectady were full of strays that sometimes formed packs when he was a boy. He'd learned as he made his deliveries to ride his bike right into them.

"Yaahh!" he yells, hurling the dirt and picking up some stones and a four-foot board from the ruins. He runs a few paces forward.

Four more dogs round the corner. They leak to the side, forming a semicircle around Joe.

Apparently a lot of dogs weren't eaten. Apparently a lot haven't been eating.

Joe retreats toward the cart, swinging the board. When the bravest dog advances, he takes a quick step forward and the dog stops.

Joe continues backing up. Several dogs crouch and creep toward him.

Joe looks behind him in time to see the older child, probably about nine years old, scoop a handful of stew into his mouth.

"Hey!" he shouts.

The child jumps down, grabs his smaller sibling's arm and flees, leaving one pail uncovered. The smell gets stronger. Joe goes around the cart, keeping it between him and the dogs.

Where the hell is Doc?

The animals edge closer. There are eight of them, most of them medium-sized, the largest a mongrel the size of a German Shepherd. Several are salivating. It won't be long before they charge.

"Yaahh!" Joe screams.

He puts down his board and hefts the open pail with both hands. Straining against the forty-pound weight, he shuffles sideways for about ten feet, drops the pail and kicks it over. Stew spills onto the street.

Joe scoots back to the cart, picking up the board again.

The dogs leap at the spill, growling at each other and wolfing down the beefy mess. They're quickly down to dirt.

First one, then another, and then all of them turn toward Joe, waiting behind the cart. He casts around for somewhere to run.

A gunshot!

And there, finally, is Doc, sprinting up the street, his hand in the air carrying a pistol.

He shoots into the air. The dogs pause.

Blamblamblam!

Dirt spurts into the air near the dogs' feet.

Blamblam!

The animals whirl and scatter into the wreckage of the surrounding block.

Joe slaps Doc on the back.

"Never knew how much I missed you."

"Jesus, Joe, don't you carry your gun?" Doc says, hands on his knees, breathing hard.

After they repair the cart, the men make it to Sam's home in less than a half hour. The boy is just coming out of the door of the old hotel.

"Sam," Joe chimes.

"At last," Doc pants.

When he sees how much food they're bringing, Sam hurries to get his mother. Aiko descends the stairs, a blanket wrapped around her and her infant. She puts her hand to her mouth.

Joe is beaming. He points to the pails, then to himself and Doc, then to her. We've brought this for you.

Aiko bows, points to the food, and waves her finger back and forth.

Joe looks puzzled. Aiko shakes her head, a painful smile stuck to her face.

Joe doesn't understand why she is refusing his gift. It doesn't take long for him to figure it out. People crowd behind Aiko on the stairs.

One person, then two, then three push Aiko aside, almost knocking her down, and rush to the cart. Others appear outside, carrying cups, bowls, pots, and other containers. Joe and Doc back away in the face of the onslaught.

People attack the pails, jostling each other and elbowing the two Americans aside. Some try to eat where they are, but they can't keep their position by the pails. Most scoop Cookie's stew as quickly as they can and make their way out of the mob, bending over their food to preserve it.

A few fights break out. One young man grapples with an older woman and takes her stew for himself. The woman shrieks. A child forces another man to drop his pot. Precious food slops onto the street.

Joe thinks of how his parents fed the neighbors from their grocery store when he was young during the Depression, how everyone made do with less, how everyone tried to be polite and orderly.

"These people … they're like the dogs," he says.

"Dog-hungry," Doc says.

Aiko stands to one side, one arm around Sam, watching. She catches Joe's eye, smiles sadly, and shrugs.

The stew is gone in less than five minutes.

9

Isamu

All the way to the train station, people know who he is. Nods from passers-by, nudges among vendors behind stalls framed by icicles, whispers floating like smoke in the chilled air.

"There's the kid who got the stew. Special delivery from the U.S. Navy."

"Why did they bring so much?"

"An officer's wife, you know. She can never get enough."

Giggles follow Isamu like mice as he scurries across the square, both arms crossed over his chest to ward off the cold and the comments he is meant to overhear.

"I hear they were handsome ..." a teasing female voice.

"So ugly ..." another woman's voice.

Isamu always relied on being small and quick, on being invisible most of the time. Now it's not possible. He's the talk of the neighborhood.

It's okay. This is the new Isamu.

He doesn't care if they stare. No more skulking, no more hiding. That's over. It's not working. The blue blotches across both cheeks prove that. He'll wear his bruises as badges, proudly, enjoying the unspoken reactions wherever he goes. If staying out of sight isn't making it, he'll try look-at-me.

His ribs are still sore and his knee stiff, but he's recovering from his beating, at least physically. But Isamu lives in fear—of hunger, of bigger boys, of being trapped. It's with him all the time.

He's got to be braver, or at least seem to be, so no one will bother him. That's what he believes. He slows his pace and lowers his arms. He won't let people see that their comments upset him. He squares his shoulders and strides through the market.

Tucked inside his trousers is a short steel rod, something the old Isamu could have used a few days ago.

He swivels his head, searching for a break, an idea, an opportunity. Nothing interesting this morning. The merchants assume he has money, but he has none. He has nothing to trade either and he's too visible to pinch anything.

He needs a new way to get by. No more Americans. They're causing problems. He's going to stay away from them. He was lucky to find those sailors when he did. That plan worked pretty well for a while, but it's getting out of control. Yesterday showed that.

One of the bigger boys who ganged up on him is leaning over a booth, brandishing a sweet potato, and intimidating a vendor. Takeo smashes his hand down on the shelf of black-market goods, spilling rice, tea, wooden clogs, and kettles onto the dirt street.

"You don't pay me," the boy smiles sweetly, "you don't stay here."

Distraught, the merchant flaps his hands and bows repeatedly. "Please, please, please."

"Do you want to stay in business?"

"I do. I do. I pay. I pay."

Takeo glances at Isamu.

"What are you looking at, *kuso?*" he laughs. "Bring us some more of that Navy grub."

Isamu wants to cower and scamper away, but he makes himself stand straight and look calmly at his tormenter. He casually continues down the aisle. He's feels like he's balanced on the edge of a deep pit, but he doesn't let it show, and Takeo turns back to the vendor.

Isamu draws a fluttery breath. He pulled it off. With a little bounce to his step, he circles toward home.

He comes upon Mama, hurrying across an ashen lot with

Hana-*chan* strapped to her back, carrying a few vegetables.

"Oh, Isamu. I'm glad to see you."

She seems so tired. She smears dirt on her face with the back of her hand.

"I took these from our plot. I was afraid to leave them in the ground. Someone will take them."

"They're awful small," the boy says, receiving them from her.

"They're better than nothing."

He's determined to declare his new role at home too. He's a little shaky, but he pushes the feeling down.

"We've got to discuss the Americans," he says, as they trudge back to their place. "Everybody's talking about them. There are a lot of nasty remarks."

"I heard them too."

"We've got to get rid of Joe and the other one," Isamu says. "It was a mistake to show them where we live."

"What will we do to eat?" Mama asks. "You can't count on the rations."

They enter their room and Isamu unties his sister and lifts her to his shoulder. Mama busies herself with arranging their meager harvest on the table.

"The garden certainly isn't going to give us what we need," she says.

"I am the man of the house," Isamu says, his voice breaking. "I will provide. You must not be troubled."

Mama purses her lips and looks away. She allows silence to build.

Isamu takes it as assent. He can feel the power shift within the family. He will be responsible. He will be the dependable one. He ignores the knot in his stomach.

"Good," he says. "It's settled."

"We are never to see the Americans again?"

"*Hai*," he barks. That's right. He sounds like his father.

"Why do you think we need to do this?"

"So people won't hate us," Isamu says. "So they won't steal from us."

Mama shakes her head.

"And Hana-*chan*? What will become of her?"

Before Isamu can answer, they hear steps rising on the stairs. Mama is moving toward the door, as heavy knocking begins.

It's Joe, unannounced, uninvited, filling the frame.

"*Konnichiwa*," he says, taking off his cap. "Hello."

He grins broadly, pleased with himself to speak Japanese, the boy assumes.

Surprised, Mama smiles, perhaps more than politely, quickly covering her mouth with her hand. She's embarrassed to be caught in her blouse and pantaloons.

She steps back, inviting the big American inside.

"Just wanted to stop by and make sure you're okay," he says. "I'm sorry we caused such a fuss."

Neither the mother nor the son can make out what the man is saying. Isamu picks out "okay" and figures from Joe's tone of voice that he's apologizing for the ruckus yesterday.

Isamu is mortified by his own behavior, by his tears at the docks the day before last. He shouldn't have let his emotions show, especially in front of the *gaijin*. He's too old for that. He sits against the wall, brooding, Hana-*chan* in his lap.

The American is so loud, he brays like a farm animal. So rude, he stomps his feet like a horse, still in his shoes.

Mama motions for him to sit, lights the fire under the teapot and drapes a scarf over her shoulders. She shoves the vegetables on the table into a bag. She still has a dirty streak on her cheek.

Joe clops across the room in his heavy shoes, tracking mud onto Mama's tatami again, and drops onto the cushion. The man is never still, constantly shifting his weight, looking around, clearing his throat.

He smiles at Isamu. He notices the framed photo of Father in his uniform and picks it up. He points to it and raises his eyebrows questioningly. Isamu looks away.

As Mama serves his tea, he points to the picture and to her and raises his eyebrows.

"Where is he?" he asks, pointing to the picture.

Mama looks down.

The American puts on a sad face, but Isamu doesn't buy it. He hasn't reached puberty yet, but he sees how Joe gazes at his mother. He understands that Joe's interest may extend beyond kindness and respect.

Father shipped out a year and a half ago and never sent any word home since then. He never met his daughter. But Mama is bound to him by her culture as strictly as if he were standing beside her. She is supposed to spend the rest of her life praying, waiting to die so she can rejoin him.

Joe reaches into his jacket and brings out a bag. More ghastly meat things.

"*Iie!*" Isamu says loudly. "*Iie!*" He shakes his head and his finger back and forth.

Joe is confused. He holds both hands open.

"Aren't they any good? What's wrong?"

Mama doesn't know how to answer. The officer's wife again, she's concerned about her guest's discomfort. She smiles graciously and holds out her hands to accept the food.

"Pah!" the boy mutters in the corner.

Mama glances at him and frowns at his rudeness.

Joe raises his cup. Mama hesitates and does the same, then bows her head.

Isamu carries the baby to his mother, then bows to Joe and walks out the door.

Enraged, he trots past the merchants in their booths, hating the mice, trying not to hear them.

He needs a new plan.

10

Joe

Four bells. Dawn over Tokyo Bay.

Salmon pink skims over the water like cursive across a page, revealing dozens of huge creatures, gunmetal gray, dozing in the gentle swells.

Prehistoric. Posthistoric.

The Allied Fleet, the destroyed city still in darkness.

Officer of the Deck on the morning watch, Joe has been on duty since 4:00 a.m., drinking mud, musing ....

... on the new world order, the winners and losers, the apparatus of the Occupation filling the harbor.

... on being a cog in a military machine 6,000 miles from home in someone else's country. In ordinary times, he'd never be here. He'd never have met her.

Scattered across his consciousness, his last few moments with Aiko. Her smile of apology after the boy stormed out, her unspilled tears as she turned away. The way she tilted her head into his hand when he took a chance and brushed the smear from her face.

"I ... I've got to see you. Can I see you?"

And she said: "Joe-*san*."

That's all. "Joe-*san*." And she put her hand over his.

He's aflame with the memory.

His moods are brittle. One moment he's unaccountably elated, another in ambushed depression for no apparent reason.

Why did the boy leave? Where did he go? Why didn't he want the sandwiches?

It's December. What happens to them in a month when the *Chourre* sails?

Why didn't he tell her he's shipping out? How can he tell her anything when everything he says must sound like gibberish to her?

Churning with worries, Joe is not very good company. He shows his short temper when the "fellas" rehash the food riot during a darkroom break.

"Ya got somethin' goin' with Sam's mom, don't ya?" Wade asks abruptly.

"No, not really. She's a woman trying to feed two children with nothing."

"Ha. Ya didn't go to all that trouble for nothin'. Ya were trying to impress her."

"You're Section 8, Wade. You don't know what you're talking about."

"I don't? Look, don't go to so much trouble. Just take what ya want."

"Maybe that's the way they do it in the big city," Joe snaps, "but not where I'm from."

"You're a long way from where ya came from."

"There's nothing you can do, Binky." Doc shakes his head. "You've got to let them go."

"I can't. I won't."

The best way to punch Joe's stubborn button (he has a big one) is to tell him he can't do something.

"I can leave them with money," he says.

"It will run out," Doc says, "sooner or later."

"I can go to GHQ and get them a job."

"For the child or the woman with a baby?"

"They'll laugh at ya," Wade says

"I've made a connection with these people," Joe says. "I can't undo it."

He is pining for her, but he decides to be with Sam. He thought he established a bond when the boy broke down in his arms. He doesn't know what happened since then to turn Sam against him, but he figures it will be easier for Aiko if he can mend his rift with her son.

He locates the sack they took from Matsushiro and removes a bat, two gloves, and several balls. He throws the baseball gear into a smaller pack and walks to Aiko's hotel. He brings his pistol, but the trip is without incident.

A rare warm day, he finds the boy outside and bawls his nickname.

"Sam!"

The boy turns, red-faced.

Joe holds up one finger, smiles, and reaches into the sack. He brings out a baseball glove.

"Ta-dah ..."

He hands it to Sam and takes out the other one.

"Put it on."

Joe demonstrates. The boy reluctantly puts his hand in the heavy leather glove.

Joe tosses a baseball, but Sam doesn't try to catch it. It falls at his feet.

Joe takes the boy's lack of enthusiasm as a personal challenge. Without missing a beat, he motions for him to throw the ball back to him and then he catches it.

"See? It's easy. You know how to do this."

He tosses another soft one. It bounces off Sam's glove.

"Throw it back."

But Sam takes off the glove and hands it to Joe. He picks up the ball and rocks it in his arms like a baby. Ball is for babies.

What a shame, Joe thinks. The kid has forgotten how to have fun. Another unforeseen wartime casualty.

Disappointed, he decides to go upstairs, but Sam grabs his sleeve. He shakes his head.

"*Iie! Iie!*"

"I just want to say hello to your mother."

The boy continues to shake his head and waves his hands. It seems important to him.

"Okay." Joe holds up his hands. "Okay."

A lot of people are watching. He realizes that he and Sam have been an entertainment. He came to make it better, not worse. He grabs the pack and gear and departs.

It is torture for him not to see her.

Undeterred, he fills a sack with cold weather supplies. As an officer, and a well-liked one at that, it's easy to access lockers stuffed with unused blankets. There are plenty on board. He finds discarded clothing that no one cares if he takes.

The next afternoon he treks by himself to Aiko's room. People peek out of their rooms at him as he strains to carry the bulging sack up the stairs.

Sam isn't there. It is a stolen moment.

They are careful with each other, formal. She bows to him. Joe bows back. She nestles the baby in her blanket.

He holds his hand at waist level. The little one. Both hands open. Where?

She doesn't know. A head shake, a wistful smile. She seems worried.

He shows her what he's brought. She is delighted. She lifts a frayed pea coat and admires it. He moves behind her to help her put it on and then closes his arms around her. She jerks away, but he holds tight and kisses her head.

She relaxes against him. He touches her chin, tenderly, raising her head, turning her toward him. They embrace, her cheek on his chest, his chin on the top of her head.

It doesn't last long, not long enough. He steps back, embarrassed by his hardness.

Laughter, very soft.

He signs. You. Me. Away.

That sad smile again.

Away, he gestures. Away.

She shakes her head, shivers.

Hana-*chan* whimpers and her mother goes to her, picks her

up.

How can he tell her he's departing in less than a month? Joe points to himself. Me. He waves his hand. Goodbye. He holds up four fingers. Four weeks. Then he makes an exaggerated frown.

Aiko doesn't understand. The little girl on her shoulder, she opens one palm and shakes her head.

Joe holds up four fingers again, but she puts her hand around his, then slides two fingers around his wedding band. She looks in his eyes and cocks her head.

Joe looks down for a long moment, then stares directly into her eyes. He holds both arms close together at full length, pointing into the distance. Far away. Then he holds his hands close to his chest and motions back and forth toward Aiko. You and I here.

The baby coughs. Aiko turns away to tend to her. She dips a towel into a bucket and squeezes water into Hana-*chan*'s mouth. She blows very softly on the infant's face.

"I can bring a bottle for her," Joe says and, when she peers over her shoulder, he signs. He points to himself, makes a giving gesture with one hand, mimes drinking from a bottle, and points to the baby.

A troubled expression on her face, Aiko turns back to the child.

Joe waits, watches. He wants to take her far from her hard life, to make her happy. At least for a few hours. He signs again and speaks at the same time.

"You. Me. Away."

His hands open, his eyes hoping.

She rocks the child. A weary smile and she nods at him.

Joe widens his eyes and raises his brows. She nods again.

A loud *Ha!* and, when she hushes him, a wide grin.

They bow to each other and Joe backs out the door, excited and awkward as a teen.

"I'll set something up," he says, knowing she doesn't comprehend. "I'll do it right away. I'll get back to you. Or I'll find a way to do that. Or ... or ... I don't know."

He laughs and she does too.

He doesn't see the people with sly grins watching him out of the corners of their eyes, as he leaves the hotel. He doesn't hear the lip smacks. He doesn't notice Sam behind the charcoal stall.

Joe is lost in his own considerations. How can he spend more time with this woman?

What does the end of the war mean to her? Bitterness? Grief? Release?

What is her life like without a husband? What will it be without him?

Where can the two of them find some privacy?

He's bouncing on an emotional pogo stick, going even higher than he did at dawn, even lower when he thinks of leaving her.

"You okay, Joe?" Doc inquires at dinner.

"Just tired ... or wired. I'm not sure which."

Doc gives him a curious look.

The following day on the forenoon watch, Joe routinely glasses the harbor, the shoreline, the piers and there's Sam slouching against a piling with his arms wrapped around himself. He seems small, even for him, but maybe it's the distance.

As soon as he's relieved at noon, Joe grabs a couple sandwiches and takes the launch ashore. As he gets closer, he can see that the boy has been beaten again.

Sam coughs and it's obvious that his ribs are sore. His wrist is bandaged. It seems to hurt him to stand, but he pushes himself erect as Joe lands.

Slowly, stiffly, he signs and Joe decodes the message.

Door. Kick.

The boy shudders and stops. He needs a few moments to compose himself.

"Is that what happened to you?" Joe asks.

Sam glares at him and nods. He mimes putting on a coat.

"Coat?" Joe says.

Sam nods again, then makes a two-handed taking motion.

"That's what they took?"

The boy nods a third time and bends over in pain. He straightens and faces Joe, brings his hands together and bows. Then he points at Joe and pushes his hands outward.

You. Stay away.

Joe opens his arms, shakes his head.

It's clear it hurts to repeat the gestures, but the boy does it anyway.

You. Away.

He turns and hobbles toward home.

11

Isamu

It takes nearly an hour to get home and every muscle and joint in his body screams at every step. He keeps his eyes down. He doesn't check around for danger. He doesn't care.

Back at the room, he eases onto his torn tatami, facing the wall, and tries to make his mind go blank. Pain zen.

The door to the room hangs by one hinge. Mama has nothing to drape over the opening, so people can look in. He doesn't care about their cruel comments.

"Look at these poor people."

"They weren't always that way."

"Why don't they fix up their place?"

Mama swept up the shattered dishes and scrubbed the stained mats, but the walls have holes kicked in them and the floor is bare where the straw was destroyed. Despair seeps like soot through the room.

And Mama? She's moving in the background, barely audible above his clamoring headache. He hears her and then he doesn't.

Later, he notices her soft step coming up the stairs and into the room. His sister is crying, big gulping sobs. So is his mother.

He doesn't care.

He sleeps and the assault recurs in his dreams. The crowd coming through the door. He couldn't stop anybody. He couldn't even delay them. They kept coming. Crawling on all fours, trying to dodge the kicks.

Ato, watching from the top of the stairs …

When he regains full consciousness, he is famished. Mama and Hana-*chan* are both asleep, huddled in the corner away from the door, shivering under Mama's scarf. He finds a raw sweet potato under his torn blanket.

He bites into it and crawls over to cover his mother and sister.

Mama rouses. He permits her to wash his face with a wet cloth, a process of sharp twinges over several minutes, despite her gentleness. She tears her scarf and wraps a clean strip around his wrist. He can see scratches on her arms.

"I was very proud of you," she tells him. "You were very brave."

He doesn't care.

When he wakes the next time, Mama is waiting for him. He manages to sit up.

"Walk with me, Isamu," she says. "I'm afraid to go alone."

"What about ..." he motions toward the door.

"There's nothing left for them to take."

He struggles to the stairs, clutching the steel rod stuffed down his trousers, one of his few remaining possessions. It didn't do him any good during the attack. He was down before he could reach it.

Isamu can barely walk at first, but it gets a little easier as they descend. Physically. It gets worse in every other way.

"There they go. They think they're Americans."

"Where's your boyfriend?"

"White man's whore!"

Mama trembles with rage. She turns her back as if she could shield Hana-*chan* from the taunts.

Isamu holds the baby, while she goes to the loo. When she returns, she walks toward the vendors.

"I'm worried about you," she tells her son. "Your body is growing and healing. You need to eat."

"If you don't eat, the baby doesn't either," he replies.

"Surely someone will take pity. Someone will give us some credit."

But no one will.

She is not the only soldier's wife who has survived by entertaining the Americans, far from it, but Mama bears the brunt of the shame for all of them. Even though she hasn't done what people assume.

"You know us," she pleads. "You know we'll pay you as soon as we can."

"For you, the price is twice as high," says a vendor wearing the pea jacket Joe gave Mama.

Isamu erupts. "Who are you to judge us? Give me that jacket!"

When the merchant scoots to the side, the boy tries to overturn the counter full of puny vegetables and tins of beans.

"Stop!" Mama cries. "Isamu, stop!" She is practically in tears.

Still sore, the boy winces as the table slams down. It hurts to care.

How will they find food? Who will feed them?

The Americans attracted too much attention. And his plan to be the new, outfront Isamu … clearly that isn't working. To survive, he and Mama need to recover their anonymity. Good citizens are seldom seen.

By the time Isamu escorts his mother and sister back to their room, he knows what he has to do.

He's getting so he can walk fairly well, so it doesn't take long before he spots one of the bigger boys by a blackened cement building that used to be a warehouse. Kiro glances around furtively before he cracks open a side door concealed by fallen timbers and slips inside.

Isamu lingers outside the door, building up courage, breathing deeply. These are the boys who hurt him. He feels those punches again, those kicks. He's afraid. He can't let them know it.

He eases the door open, slowly, as silently as he can, and steps inside.

Pitch black.

One step, his hand in front of him.

Two.

His eyes adjust. He can make out clumps of heavy-looking equipment and stacks of boxes.

Step three.

He sees someone coming toward him out of the dimness.

"Didn't you get enough last week, Navy Boy?"

Ato is tall and slender with an air of menace. His ravaged face wears a toxic sneer.

Someone pushes back a curtain and dirty light filters into the vast room. Isamu can see several other youths lounging against the heavy masses, watching him. One sharpens a knife. Another slaps a club across his open palm.

Isamu is grateful the murk hides his trembling.

"I want in," he says as boldly as he can.

"So you can tell your monster friends all about us?" Ato mocks.

"I ... I ... I want to get rid of the Americans as much as you do."

"You went to the port," Takeo accuses. "You served them. You helped the monsters."

"No. I was just ... taking their money. I ... I was starving."

"Everybody is starving," Ato says. "That's what they've done to us."

Chunky Kiro snickers. "They brought you all that crap."

"I didn't ask them to bring it. They came when I wasn't there."

"And you kept it all for yourself," Kiro says.

"No, I ... "

"What a selfish thing to do when your brothers here could use some warm things," Ato says.

The other boys chuckle and mutter assent.

"Somebody needed to be taught a lesson," Takeo says.

Isamu looks up at Ato.

"Is that why you just stood there and let it happen?"

"Why did you fight?" The slender youth's smile creases his scar.

Isamu looks down again.

"What do I have to do to join?"

"Bring us the American."

"I can't. I told him to stay away. He caused this."

He waves his bandaged wrist, touches a nick on his face.

"Change your mind," Ato insists.

"I can't."

"Sure you can. He obviously has some attraction to your room. I don't think it's you."

Ugly laughter.

Ato nods and Takeo reaches into a bin and hands Isamu some orange peels and a couple soft potatoes with sprouts growing on them. Isamu wrinkles his nose in distaste.

"What do you say?" Takeo asks.

"Thank you," Isamu mutters.

He hurries home with his paltry meal. As he nears the hotel, two military men emerge, one American and one Japanese, carrying the damaged door to his room. They load it into the back of a jeep parked around the corner.

At the top of the stairs behind a new door, Isamu discovers his mother, sitting on the floor bent over Hana-*chan*.

"Mama?"

She looks up, smiling and wiping her eyes. Was she crying?

"Did those soldiers come here?"

She nods. "Joe-*san* sent them."

She seems a little off-balance. The men in uniforms, their big boots and noisy tools, perhaps they agitated her.

"It's a fine door," she says. "They patched the walls too." She begins to cry.

"Is something wrong, Mama?"

"No. Everything is fine. I'm pleased." She stands and wipes her eyes. "I don't know why I'm tearing up."

The floor is muddy, which she normally can't stand, but she ignores it. She busies herself by pulling out food and wipes for Hana-*chan*, making little piles.

He watches her for a few moments and then gives her the

orange peels and soft potatoes.

"Oh, how nice. Where did you get this?"

She places them in one of their few unbroken containers. She can't seem to settle down.

"Mama, the Americans …" the boy begins.

She walks over and folds him into a hug.

"We are so lucky," she says. "He doesn't have to help us. He chooses to do it. What would we do without him?"

He's never seen her like this before, so flighty, floaty. She returns to her fussing, arranging some clothing, and brushes some papers onto the floor. He bends to help her.

"Mama, what are these? Are these tickets?"

"Yes, they are. Let me have them. I'm going on a short trip. I need you to help me."

"You're going to see him."

"Yes. Yes, I am."

"You're packing, aren't you? That's what you're doing."

She cocks her head and turns back to the clothing.

"I know where you're going," Isamu says. "I know what you're going to do."

"I'm going to Fuji. That's where the American wants to go."

"The people on the street, they already call you names, Mama."

"All the more reason to get away from here."

"Mama, I … I can't allow it."

"Isamu," she says softly. "I'm not asking permission. I'm asking you to watch your sister for a few hours. Overnight."

"This isn't necessary," Isamu says. "There are things I can do. There are things I'm doing." How can he tell her what Ato wants?

"Look at you. Look at your face," Mama insists. "I know you want to take care of us, but you can't do it all by yourself."

"You don't have to do this."

"It's important … for our family."

"I've seen the way you look at him," Isamu says.

Mama is changing the baby's rags. She stops and glances up at him sharply.

"I am your mother and you will never speak to me that way," she says.

Isamu drops his eyes.

"I hate leaving Hana-*chan*," Mama says. "I don't like putting this burden on you."

"I can take care of her. You know I can."

"I still don't like it. I've left some milk. It should be enough."

She crosses to her son, takes his chin in her hand, and stares straight into his eyes.

"You must promise me that you'll stay inside the room until I get back, that you will never leave her."

He nods, looks down.

"He will take care of us, Isamu. You'll see."

12

Joe

It isn't an easy drive. The roads are full of potholes. The encampments spill into the right-of-way all along the thrashed suburbs. In some sections, Joe has to slow to a crawl to avoid hitting someone.

There are children everywhere, more and more as he gets farther from the city. When they spot the jeep, some of them rush toward it. Joe shakes his head and waves them away. He didn't bring any gum or candies.

It's difficult to concentrate. His mind is a whirlpool with Aiko in the center, all his thoughts circling her.

He feels her hand close over his fingers, hears her near-whisper: "Joe-*san*."

It draws him on. It keeps him from turning around in the face of the enormous suffering scattered on the waysides. He doesn't want to see any more of it. He'd rather go back into his little metal cubbyhole and calculate batting averages.

There's plenty to do, God knows. As the departure date nears, his duties aboard ship increase. There's a spike in radio communications: instructions on how to navigate out of the crowded harbor, logistical information, orders about the long voyage back across the Pacific.

He's got to make her understand that he's leaving. He wants their relationship to be honest, not to be based on false expectations. At least they can have a few weeks to be together.

The jeep jounces over a rock ... *not a kid, please not a kid* ... and almost stalls. Joe feathers the gas and the engine backfires, but keeps running. He glances behind him, relieved that there's no one in the road.

A lot of backfires lately. He tried to help Aiko and Sam, but he got them in trouble. The food he brought made them a target. His gifts attracted thieves and thugs.

He hopes he's not doing it again, setting them up for more problems.

You. Me. Away.

He was fearful that Aiko was injured, but the Navy carpenter's mate told him she was all right. She's got a better door and patched walls, but her room is still bare.

Sam told him to stay away. He's honored the boy's request, technically, although he arranged for the repairs and the ticket delivery. But now he's stealing the boy's mother, at least for a short while.

He's been checking every day, but there's been no sign of Sam on the pier. What's going on with him? What can Joe do to regain his confidence? He doesn't want to leave the country with bad feelings between them. He likes the boy, feels protective toward him. He's impressed with his energy and intelligence.

This is his first trip without him as the guide, Joe reflects, as he begins a winding climb into colder country. He stops and zips the windows closed on the canvas top and consults Wade's map.

Without the help of his friends he'd never be able to pull off an adventure like this.

Cookie asked his brother, the carpenter's mate, who's stationed aboard another ship in Tokyo Bay. He traded a generous serving of stew for the new door and its installation.

Doc knew somebody who knew somebody.

"I went to school with the exec aboard *Alabama* and he's got a brother in GHQ," he said. "Let me see what I can do."

The result: a round-trip train ticket for Aiko, so she would be spared the embarrassment of traveling with an American, plus one luxury room at the base of Mount Fuji.

You. Me. Away.

Gaining elevation, the shoulders of the road fall away to evergreens and ravines, leaving no room for makeshift shacks.

Joe catches his first glimpse of majestic Fuji, far in the distance.

It's Wade's contribution that makes him smile.

Joe couldn't tell Cookie where Aiko's room is. He doesn't even know her last name. His plan couldn't work if no one could find Sam and Aiko.

"Jesus, Binky, ya totally lost it with this lady, haven't ya?" Wade observed when Joe unloaded to the "fellas." "Ya look like hell."

Prints hanging in the darkroom showed Christmas decorations in the windows of buildings in Little America. Wade was onshore most days, taking shots of various Tokyo neighborhoods.

"They live over by the train station, don't they?" Wade asked. "I've been in that neighborhood. Gimme a description of the hotel and I'll get the address for ya."

Joe was surprised. He'd expected to take some told-you-sos from the photographer.

"What?" Wade says. "I'm not always a jerk, ya know."

For good measure, he added: "Stupid Nips. They shoulda told ya where ya were."

He also found a good map and detailed driving directions to Mount Fuji. He traded watches so Joe could disappear overnight and loaned him the jeep assigned for "official photography."

A wide turn reveals Fuji across a broad lake, its reflection splintered by drifting ice.

You. Me. Away.

Driving down twisting curves, he can see shanties at the side of the highway again, people in thin pajamas, their breaths visible. Fat white flakes begin to fall from the sky.

What has he gotten himself into? What about his wife? A stab of guilt, quickly suppressed. What began as a casual friendship with the boy has become something complex and compelling, a vessel he does not captain bound for an unknown destination. Too late to turn back now.

He waits at the depot, surrounded by signs of destruction.

A burned-out boxcar sits on a siding. Two sheds, now charred shells, slowly fill with snow. Next to a fifteen-foot pile of debris are several lean-tos, blankets across the open sides.

He doesn't know if she will come. His gut clenches as the train heaves into view. He feels like the steam puffing out of the smokestack.

He watches the passengers unload, pouring down the rickety stairs, dropping out of windows, leaping off the couplings between cars. So many people.

Joe doubts she will be among them. There are many reasons for her not to be aboard: Sam, the baby, the weather, the war. Maybe she doesn't want to meet him. Even if she does, she probably resisted the temptation.

The throng on the platform thins. She isn't there. He's about to turn away.

Then he sees a small figure, standing by the last car. She's dressed entirely in black and she has no luggage. So tiny. Could it be …

It is! There she is!

He waves. She wiggles her fingers at him.

They walk toward each other. He wants to break into a run and sweep her into his arms, but he restrains himself. He's the only American at the station. He doesn't want to make her uncomfortable in public.

They converge and press their palms together. They hold each other's eyes for a few moments, as the train, the smoke, and the other people swirl around them,

It is so cold and yet they are flushed.

When they step back, she smiles and gestures at the snow-capped peak, *Fuji-san*, shy as a maiden behind veils of clouds. He doesn't even look. He can only see her.

She checks directions at the ticket window. They drive to the inn and she waits in the jeep, while Joe passes under the distinctive triangular roof and checks in.

It is a traditional ryokan, very different from hotels back in the States. The floor of their room is covered with tatami mats like Aiko's apartment. There are no dressers, no chairs, no bed. Several cushions surround a low wooden table.

Aiko removes her shoes and signals for Joe to do the same. She goes to a cupboard and removes paper slippers. They're too small for Joe.

The room is so cold they can see their breaths, but there is a squat brazier loaded with coals. While Joe kneels and lights it, Aiko opens another cupboard and pulls out a futon and some linens, which she arranges in the center of the space.

She goes behind a rice paper screen. Her clothing appears over the light wooden frame. She emerges in a patterned robe. She hands a second robe to Joe ..."yukata"... and gestures at the screen.

He strips behind the screen and tries on the robe. The sleeves come to his elbows. The fabric reaches to his knees and barely closes around him.

Aiko tries to hide her smile with a hand in front of her mouth.

For the next too-few hours, they're together. They are not Japanese and American. Just man and woman.

Just Joe. Just Aiko.

They don't speak much. Words aren't important to them. They communicate with their hands.

At first they're tentative, eager and scared at once. She sits on the futon, facing away, head down, as if ashamed. Then she arches her neck, wriggles her toes.

He lowers himself next to her. He feels like an awkward, oversized child in undersized clothing, crawling on his hands and knees.

He puts one arm around her and holds her. Gently, she lays her head on his shoulder. She is tense.

Joe releases her and stretches full-length on the mat behind her. He pushes gently on her back and then lets up. As she leans back, he takes her shoulder and guides her down next to him. She pulls up her legs and turns away.

He snugs behind her and puts his arm around her. She is so small, doll-like. She smells so good. Slowly, she relaxes.

If this is all that happens, he thinks, it's worth it. This will be enough.

But it isn't. His body insists. He moves back a little. He doesn't want to pressure her with his erection. But she moves back, too.

She turns to him, puts her hands in his hair, on his face. She stares at him with a serious look. They barely know each other.

They learn quickly. She opens his robe. Hers falls open as she moves atop him. He can feel her ribs, taste the trace of Tokyo on her skin, the faint scent of ash.

A patient man, given to slowness in sexual matters, Joe understands that her pleasure is his. She isn't used to that. He seems to surprise her.

"Joe-*san*!"

She surprises him, as well. They have much to teach each other. It is a mutual surrender and occupation of the heart. It seems endless, yet it is over in an instant.

He never finds a way to tell her he's going home.

13

Isamu

He doesn't want to stay with his baby sister, but Mama gave him no choice. He spends the night behind the new door with the strong locks, safe and private. He promised he'd stay until Mama returns.

When Hana-*chan* gets hungry, he dips a rag in the jar of breast milk that Mama left behind and lets her suck it dry, patiently repeating the process until she's full.

From master of the house to babysitter, it feels like a demotion and it hurts his pride. How can he provide for the family if he's stuck inside with Hana-*chan*? Maybe he doesn't have as much power in their little kingdom as he thought.

Yet Mama is trusting him to care for the baby for the first time, so it's also a promotion. Confusing.

He takes his assignment seriously. He stares at the child. He's never had her to himself for so long. Mama has him hold her sometimes, but she always takes her back in a few minutes.

He notices the way she watches the cold draft shifting the flimsy curtain Mama put over the window, her eyes following the foldings and openings, the light and shadow from the flickering oil lamp.

How helpless she is. How much she depends on others. Her mother. Her father ... she never knew him. Can a brother be a father?

Can Joe?

Mama has been different the last few days. She sings to Hana-*chan*. She hasn't done that since the firebombing.

Is Joe the reason?

His head swimming, Isamu nods off. The baby is already asleep.

He wakes before dawn to her hungry screams. Crossing the room in the darkness, he stumbles and shatters the milk jar.

He tries to get the baby to take some rice gruel, but she refuses. He manages to drip some water into her mouth, but she won't stop crying. No amount of rocking her does any good. He'll have to replace the milk.

Not easy. Milk is difficult to find, even on the black market. Isamu knows of one place near the train station that carries it.

He wraps Hana-*chan* in rags to keep her warm, puts her in the burlap sack and ties her to his back. He stuffs the steel bar down his trouser leg. At the last second, he grabs a cup.

The sun is just coming up as he steps outdoors, a slight boy with a baby on his back, small puffs of breath visible before and behind. Hana-*chan* is still wailing.

Shivering in the cold, Isamu scuttles across the square. Merchants are rolling up their awnings by the time he gets to the stall. The milk is in a five-gallon jug behind the counter.

"Please," he holds out his cup to the vendor. "For my sister."

The man names an impossible price.

"Just a little 'til my mother comes back."

"Get away."

He removes the steel bar from his pants and waves it in the air.

"I don't want to hurt you."

The merchant laughs. He reaches under the counter and removes a club twice the size of Isamu's.

Isamu puts the bar back in his pants. He unhooks his sack and sets the squalling infant on the counter.

"You've got to help me," he pleads.

"If I give my goods away," the man answers, "who will help me?"

"I'll give you the sack," Isamu says over the baby's cries.

The vendor stares at him for a moment, then looks at the baby and nods.

"Let me have your cup."

Isamu takes Hana-*chan* out of the burlap and offers it to the merchant. He waves it off.

"Thank you," the boy says. "I'll find a way to repay you."

He sits by the side of the booth and dips a rag in the cup to feed the baby. When she's finished, he settles her in one arm and carries the partially filled cup in the other hand.

He's on his way home when Kiro startles him, talking in his ear before Isamu even knows he's there.

"Come with me," the chunky boy says.

"I've got to get my sister home."

"Come now."

A few minutes later at the warehouse, Isamu says the same thing to Ato.

"I've got to get my sister home."

"No wonder you haven't delivered the American," the scar-faced boy sneers.

"What are you talking about?" Isamu asks.

"She took the train to Fuji," Ato says. "She met him there."

"I trailed her," Takeo boasts. "The slut."

"You shut up!" Isamu shouts.

Hana-*chan* begins to cry again. He hugs his sister to him.

"You're playing games with us, Navy Boy," Ato says.

"And after we were so nice to you," says Kiro, bubbling laughter.

"It's not true," Isamu says. "I'll do what I promised. I'll bring him to you. I just haven't had the chance."

Ato snaps his fingers and a girl steps forward.

"Keiko, take the child," Ato says. "Shut it up."

Isamu tries to hold on, but Kiro grabs his arms and the girl gets the baby.

"I won't hurt her," Keiko says. "We have milk."

"I can't leave her here," Isamu pleads.

"You've got no choice," Takeo chuckles.

"Find the American and bring him here," Ato says. "This is your last chance."

Isamu doesn't go back to the room. He doesn't want to face Mama, not without Hana-*chan*. He crosses the barren blocks as rapidly as he can, his thoughts roiling as he runs.

Things are spinning out of control. He never meant to put Mama in an awkward position, to get her involved with Ato and his gang. He certainly doesn't mean to hurt her. But he will, if he turns over Joe.

He doesn't have a good feeling about that. The American tried to help, even though it led to trouble. The boy doesn't want to harm him. What will Ato do to him?

What choice does he have? What else can he do to get his sister back?

Then he has an idea. Maybe there is a way nobody has to get hurt …

He arrives at the docks winded, perspiring despite the frigid temperature. There are no sailors in the vicinity. Isamu stands at water's edge, waving his arms.

The wind whips off Tokyo Bay. It's bitter cold.

A small craft with four sailors in it pushes off from the *Chourre*. Joe is not among them. The men are all wearing round white caps. Isamu accosts them as soon as they land, jabbering at them in a strained voice.

The men shake their heads and one holds his hands open in question.

Isamu cradles an imaginary baby in his arms and then points back across the tracts.

"Somethin' about a baby? I don't know what he wants," says a paunchy sailor.

"Joe? Joe? Joe?" the boy asks urgently.

The paunchy sailor scowls.

Isamu holds his hand to his mouth and pretends to take a bite.

"The guy with the sandwiches?" the sailor asks. "Joe? Joe Bienkunski?"

Isamu goes nuts.

14

Joe

Everything is acutely clear, but oddly disconnected.

He didn't get any sleep last night and, when he drags back in midmorning, Joe finds dozens of important communications demanding his attention. He keeps a coffee cup within reach.

He can't get Aiko out of his mind. He's full of her, the scent of her hair, the feel of her skin, the sound of her soft sighs. When can he see her again? How?

New orders are in. There's a carrier stranded in the Pacific that needs help. *Chourre* ships out late tomorrow. Tomorrow.

He's got to tell her. Without delay.

When can he get away? He needs to decode all the cables and to get the information to the proper people. He tries to concentrate, but a sense of unreality overtakes him. He imagines Aiko naked in this room. What could they do in this cramped space? They'd find something.

He makes mistakes and has to start over. He takes another swig of mud. His caffeine hum makes him jittery, but it keeps him awake.

Aiko. Fuji.

The door opens and a sailor hands him another batch of dispatches. He forces himself to focus. It's up to him to make sense of those meaningless sequences of numbers and letters. No one else can do it.

Cookie barges in.

"Sorry, Lieutenant, but there's a Jap kid out there looking for you. He's pretty upset."

Joe rubs his puffy eyes and stifles a yawn.

"Any idea what he wants?"

"Something about a baby, I think," Cookie says. "It's hard to tell what his hand motions mean."

"Oh, God. Give me five to grab some things."

He grabs his coat and stuffs a few other items in a canvas sack. He gives a sailor a sheaf of decrypted messages to deliver to the old man.

"I won't be gone long," he hears himself saying. "Too much to do to get ready for tomorrow."

They meet in the galley, where Cookie is packing some sandwiches, and pile into the launch. Joe sits in the bow, his tiredness blowing away in the chill spray, and watches the boy on shore getting nearer.

It's midday as they arrive at the docks, where Sam has been waiting with the other three enlisted men.

As soon as Joe steps ashore, the boy starts to sign, moving his hands frantically, pointing, weeping. He's shivering with cold and fear.

Joe gets the general idea. Bigger boys have taken Hana-*chan*.

"Where's your mother?" he asks.

Sam looks puzzled.

"Aiko? Where's Aiko?"

The boy points back toward home, then at himself and then at Joe. She told me to get you.

Joe shakes his head, worried. He translates for the other sailors.

Sam isn't finished. He continues to pantomime. Big boys. Blankets. Money. Cradled baby. Handed to Joe.

"What?" Cookie asks.

The boy repeats his gestures.

"I think he's saying they want blankets and money for the baby," Joe says. "A ransom demand."

"How much money?" Cookie asks. "How many blankets."

Joe rubs his fingers together. Sam holds up ten fingers five times.

"Fifty dollars," Joe says.

He mimes a blanket and a question, then counts as the boy raises ten fingers three times. Thirty.

The boy points at the sun and signs to go, to go, to go. He pulls on Joe's sleeve. The officer holds up his hand. Wait. Calm down.

"Everybody wants to help," Cookie says.

"That's not going to happen," Joe replies. "I appreciate the offer, but I don't want you men getting into any trouble."

"In all due respect, Lieutenant. We're not letting you handle this by yourself."

Joe thinks for a few moments.

"All right. You men go back to the ship and gather the blankets. Do you think we can find that many on board?"

Cookie nods. "Oh, sure. Totally doable. Ship's stores have plenty."

"Okay. Then talk to Doc Stephens about the money. Tell him I need a loan. And ask Lieutenant Wade if he can bring the stuff over in the jeep. We'll go ahead and wait at the hotel. He knows where it is."

He removes an extra jacket from the canvas bag and gives it to the boy. He takes out a pistol, which he straps to his waist.

"And tell Lieutenant Wade to throw the field phone in the back," Joe adds, handing the empty canvas to the cook. "It's in the crypto room."

It starts to snow as he and the boy set off on foot across the wasteland. The landscape strikes Joe as fantastic, the beautiful falling flakes in cruel contrast to the destruction they conceal. The surroundings are as surreal as the situation he finds himself in.

He's come all the way across the Pacific without seeing battle. *Chourre* had never come closer than a few hours away from naval combat. Now here he is advancing into harm's way in aid of ... the enemy? It's difficult to think about the boy next to him that way.

And Aiko? She's no foe. If he knows anything in this mixed-up world, he knows that.

They proceed quickly, the boy several steps ahead, and reach Sam's neighborhood in about ten minutes. Joe turns toward the hotel, but Sam tries to pull him in the other direction.

"Mama!" Joe says. "We've got to find your Mama."

The boy shakes his head and points toward the open-air market. Joe has never been there before.

"The jeep will meet us over there," Joe insists, pointing toward the room and pretending to steer a vehicle.

Aiko materializes out of the snow swirling around them. She's frantic, windblown hair everywhere. She holds Sam at arm's length, shaking him a little, a stricken look on her face, speaking intensely.

Joe doesn't know what she's saying, but he hears her baby's name? Sam gabbles a long reply. He looks scared.

Joe understands enough. The boy lied to him. He hasn't told his mother about his sister.

He feels like an intruder. She has barely glanced at him. He can see how upset she is, how she grips the boy's shoulders, how she wipes her tears.

He touches her shoulder and motions toward their home. She looks up like she just noticed him and slowly stands. She keeps an arm around her son.

Wade skids to a stop in front of the hotel.

"Sorry I'm so late," he says. "Had to go the back way 'cause of the roads."

"Got everything? The phone?"

"As ordered, Mr. B," Wade says, handing Joe a wad of cash. "Ya got a hostage situation here?"

"Afraid so. Let's go see what we can do."

Joe piles into the front seat and Sam climbs into the back, next to a stack of blankets. Joe gently stops Aiko from getting in and points to the hotel entrance. She shakes her head. She doesn't budge.

"She's not going to wait here," Joe says.

Wade shrugs. "Not a good idea, but what the hell."

15

Isamu

They jounce across the potholed streets. Isamu folds Mama into the military jacket Joe gave him to keep her warm, but doesn't answer her whispered queries. Joe speaks quickly to Wade.

The market is mostly empty. The weather has driven away the vendors, but Kiro sees them coming and ducks inside the warehouse.

They pause outside. Joe signs to the boy: "Tell them to bring the baby."

Isamu knocks and slips in the door.

In short order, the door reopens. Inside, Ato stands behind Keiko, the girl holding Hana-*chan* in her arms. He holds a knife to the infant's throat.

"Oh!" Mama cries, then puts her hand to her mouth, afraid her voice will make the baby struggle.

Joe steps out and takes a step forward, gesturing toward the jeep. "We've got what you want."

None of the gang members responds. Even if they understood the words, the American's statement wouldn't make sense to them because they never heard of the ransom.

"What is he saying?" Ato asks Isamu, standing next to him.

"I … I think they brought something for you," Isamu says. His plan appears to be working.

Joe motions to Wade, who lifts several bundles of blankets from the back of the jeep and stacks them in front of the warehouse. The boys inside the building jostle to see outside.

Joe takes the cash out of his pocket, raises it in the air and points it at the baby.

"They want to make a deal," says Isamu.

"I'm not stupid, Navy Boy."

"Think what you can do with all that," Isamu says.

Ato motions with the knife for Joe to come closer.

Joe shakes his head and points at the infant.

Joe and Ato study each other. The moment lengthens. Mama waits, attentive to Hana-*chan*'s every breath.

The second American goes back to the jeep and hoists the backpack containing the portable phone onto the passenger seat. He glances at Joe and winks.

Ato eyes both Americans, the pile of bedding, the military vehicle with the strange equipment, and the money. More than he bargained for. Snow whitens the mound of blankets. Hana-*chan* begins to cry.

"She's cold or she's hungry," Mama calls to the girl with her child.

"Or she needs a change," Keiko says, wrinkling her nose and holding the baby away from her body.

"I'll take her," Isamu offers, glancing back at Ato.

Ato laughs and pricks Hana-*chan* on the arm. A tiny trickle of blood begins to flow. Mama gasps.

Very deliberately, first Joe and then the other American reach inside their jackets, remove pistols and train them on Ato. Joe waves the money again.

Isamu watches anxiously. Despite her stink, unexpectedly, he experiences a billow of love for his sister. But he's the reason she's at knifepoint. He's the one who brought her here. He's supposed to be the man of the house. He's got to do something.

"Let her go," he begs. "I'll do anything you want."

"Tell the Americans to put down their guns. I'll trade her for him," he nods toward Joe. "He's the one I wanted all along."

Isamu signs to Joe. He lowers his gun and nods to Wade to do the same. Joe tosses his weapon to Wade, tucks the cash in his pocket, raises his arms, and takes several steps forward.

Takeo glides out the door and forces Joe's arms behind his back. Ato loosens his grip and lowers the baby to Isamu. The boy hustles her to the jeep.

"Oh my baby, my baby." Aiko wraps herself around her child, ignoring the odor.

Ato grabs Joe by the shirt and yanks him inside the warehouse, beckoning for Isamu to join them.

There are a dozen other boys scattered around the dim interior. Shafts of sunlight illuminate stacks of boxes. At Ato's instructions, the boys put Joe in a chair and tie his arms behind his back.

Ato steps forward, reaches into Joe's side pocket and takes out the cash.

"Helpless! The monster is powerless," he shouts into the American's face. "You bastard! You murderer! Ha!"

Consumed by hate, he struts in his triumph.

"How does it feel to be totally at our mercy? Now you know what it was like for us."

Ato strikes Joe open-handed across the face.

"How does it feel to be defenseless?"

Ato steps back and the other boys come forward. They circle the chair, screaming at the American.

"Monster!"

"Worm!"

"*Kuso!*"

They spit at him, flick him with their fingers. They threaten him with knives.

Isamu looks away, disgusted and frightened. He doesn't want this. He wanted the American to stay away from him and his family, but he doesn't want him hurt, especially after he returned and rescued Hana-*chan*. He's battered with conflicting feelings of loathing and horror, shame and gratitude.

Joe takes all the hits, the spit, the knife pricks without a word. It goes on for long minutes. The American looks straight ahead and tries not to react to the insults.

Finally, Takeo kicks the chair over. A bruise blooming on his cheek, Joe mumbles something in a low voice.

Ato shushes his boys. The American keeps repeating the same phrase.

"What's he saying?" Ato asks Isamu.

"I can't tell. Untie his hands."

They sit the chair upright and surround him before they untie one hand. Joe rubs his jaw gingerly. Then he holds an imaginary phone to his ear, points toward the door, and smiles through swollen lips. He does it again.

What does he mean? Ato looks at Isamu.

"A telephone?" Isamu guesses. "Out there?" That backpack the second American had?

A hint of disquiet passes over Ato's horribly scarred features.

"Kiro," he says. "Check on those blankets. Go get 'em."

Kiro doesn't want to leave the circle around Joe, but he does as he's told. He opens the door and a shocked expression pops onto his face.

"Two more jeeps out there," he says. "Lots of Americans. Lots of guns."

"*Fakku!*" Ato screams, kicking Joe in the side. "Let's get out of here! Head for the windows in back."

He leads his gang deep into the big, cluttered building, leaving Isamu to help the American to free his other arm.

16

Joe

There's no time alone, no place out of the weather. Snow feathers everything, the roof of the jeep, the streets, the blanket Aiko wears over her shoulders and her baby. She won't let go of Hana-*chan*. There is no way to embrace with the infant between them, no way to melt into each other.

Still she is radiant. In her relief at having her family whole again, her elation at seeing him, the excitement of what transpired, she shines in her own light.

They stand apart from the others, Sam watching closely, the men from the *Chourre* turned away. Gently, she touches his purpled cheek.

And Joe has to tell her.

He points to himself. Me. To the other Navy men. We.

He makes waves with his hand. Sail. She blinks against the falling flakes.

He turns his hand over, the sign they developed between them (Was that only yesterday?) for tomorrow.

Me. We. Sail. Tomorrow.

Her gentle smile dissolves, her eyes pool.

He holds his hands open, near tears himself.

As if Joe had hit a switch, her glow gutters and goes out. She makes the tomorrow sign. She points to him, then points away, far away, a stricken look on her face.

Joe nods.

She shakes her head violently, tears flying into the storm. She pushes him. She backs away and slips, almost drops the baby in her arms.

Joe lurches toward her, but she regains her balance and turns her back on him, sobbing silently. Joe comes up behind her, but she steps away from him.

A curtain of cold between them. Pain drifting down.

He looks over at the boy and smiles sadly. Sam glares at him.

Joe gestures over and over: I'm sorry. Sorry. Sorry.

The boy is unmoving in the snow, his hair whitened. A little old man, lost. What will happen to him? Who will take care of the three of them?

Joe is overwhelmed with love, with worry, with indignation at the unfairness. This is their final time together. She is so beautiful. How can he leave her? Why can't he stay?

But he knows he can't. Cookie is tugging at his arm.

I've got to go, Joe signs. Sorry. He climbs into Cookie's vehicle.

Wade gently guides Aiko toward his jeep. They depart in different directions and she turns to give Joe a last, bleak look.

On the way back to the docks, Cookie and his men regale Joe with the confusion of getting together for the adventure, the wild hunt all over the ship to grab blankets, the scare when no one could find Doc at first to get the money, the maneuvering to get several men ashore the day before they ship out. It's all fun to them, just a way to display their affection for the young officer.

"Did you see the look on that kid's face when he opened the door to that warehouse?" Cookie howls.

"I think he had some second thoughts," another seaman chuckles.

Joe pastes a smile on his kisser and laughs with the rest of them, but inside he's the amazing aching man.

"Why didn't you wait until we got here, Lieutenant?" Cookie asks.

"I was afraid they wouldn't let the baby go, if they saw all of you," Joe says. "I figured I had to get that done by myself."

He hurts pretty much everywhere, his head, his shoulders, his arms, the extremely tender side where he was kicked, his heart.

Financially, he's out fifty bucks. Ato and his boys got away with the cash, though the men are bringing the blankets back with them.

Emotionally, Joe feels like he's been pulled inside-out. All he wants to do is sleep, but that's not going to be for a while.

They skid and swerve onto the piers and clamber aboard the launch that will take them back to the ship and to work. Piles and piles of work.

Joe has so much to do. Everyone has been covering for him. The crypto room is piled with coded communiqués. He hardly has time to think before he submerges in his duties.

He surfaces after dark, bleary and mud-buzzy, and meets Doc in the galley.

"Christ, Binky," his friend had already heard. "That was so stupid. You could've got killed."

Geez. So much for sympathy. After he helped set up Fuji too. Just a couple days ago.

That time thing again. It's getting slippery for Joe. His thoughts blur, the now and the then, the here and the there.

Aiko … her head on a pillow …

Aiko … the shape of her leg …

Aiko … her hair brushing his chest …

He falls asleep sitting up, the decoding machine his hard pillow.

He wakes from a dream of Ato and his gang hammering and hammering, trying to break into Aiko's room. The sound is someone knocking on the door to the crypto room. It's Wade, returning to ship after snapping a few last shots ashore.

"The kid's out there," he tells Joe. "I left the launch for you."

His bruised face smudged with ink, Joe rubs the sleep from his eyes with the heel of his hand.

"Thanks."

He can only spare a half hour to see the boy. What does he want? Doesn't he know he's leaving today?

It's cold outside. It seems like it's always cold in Tokyo. It's warmer in the middle of the ocean than it is in this shattered city. At least it's stopped snowing, though the piers are covered in white, the boy's footprints partially filled in.

"How's Hana-*chan*?" Joe approaches and mimes holding a baby. "How's Mama?"

The boy doesn't answer. He stands wide-footed, livid, regarding Joe with scorn. His gestures are abrupt, agitated.

He points to Joe, to himself, holds his hands wide. What about me?

Joe shrugs and opens his hands. What do you mean?

Sam repeats the gestures, adds a wave of his arm toward home. What about us?

Joe opens his hands, shakes his head. I'm sorry. He points toward the ship. I have to go there.

The boy insists, opening his arms again, pointing back. He acts offended, as if Joe had done something bad to him. Maybe he had.

Joe shakes his head, points to the ship again. Not my choice, but he has no way to say that to the boy.

Sam points to Joe, to himself, to home, gestures to come on. Come back with me.

I'm sorry.

He thinks of his wife and toddler back in the States. Feels sad, tired. The shiny patch of skin on his jaw stings.

The boy points to himself, then back toward home, then sweeps his arm to the ship. Take us with you.

Joe shakes his head sadly. "I wish I could." No way to sign that either.

Sam raises opened hands, stomps his foot. Why not?

Joe touches his uniform. He salutes. My obligation.

The boy explodes. He rushes at Joe and pummels him in the belly with both fists.

"Whoa, whoa, whoa!" Joe says, grabbing Sam's hands.

The boy's rage subsides like a balloon losing air. He looks away, frees one arm and sweeps it toward the ruins.

"I'm so sorry," Joe says. "I really am."

He realizes he's come to care for the boy. He'll never forget him, will always compare his own son to him. He has so much he wants to say to him.

I wish I didn't have to go.

I wish I could stay with your mother.

I wish I could be your father.

I wish, I wish, I wish …

He's the communications officer for a U.S. naval vessel and yet he can't even express himself to a child. It's maddening that he's can't do more for him.

The boy's expression is desolation. He leaves without another word. Joe watches him recede across the blasted blocks and then, in a blink, not be there.

On the way back to the *Chourre*, Joe knows he can't leave it that way.

He checks the crypto room. The stack of messages isn't too bad, nothing that looks urgent.

He takes a few minutes to gather items and fill a canvas sack. He grabs a pair of sturdy high-tops in the smallest size and, because he knows they'll still be too large, three pairs of Navy-issue socks.

He adds two blankets rolled and tied with twine, meat and bread for a week (no time for sandwiches), some more money, and a few other items.

At the last minute, he decides to throw in more shoes. He puts in his own second pair and begs extras from Doc and Wade.

"Joe …" Doc says. "Don't do it. You're not thinking with your head."

"This is not an ending I can accept," Joe says.

"We leave at about 1800. Gangplank up about an hour earlier," Wade says. "If you're not back in time, you're in big,

big trouble."

Brig trouble, Joe thinks. As a seaman, not a lieutenant.

"I've got better than three hours," he says.

"It won't do any good," Doc says. "It won't help her."

"If you saw a burn victim, you wouldn't turn away, would you?"

Joe ducks and takes their shoes, boards the waiting launch. As soon as he sits down, he begins to doze, but the cold spray keeps waking him up. It seems like every inch of him throbs with low-grade pain.

"Look for me about 1600 hours," he tells the seaman as he starts across the flattened tracts.

People huddled around small fires watch from their inadequate shelters, a single American tracking through the new snow, hauling a heavy gray bag.

No jeep this time. Just Joe-power. He moves as quickly as he dares, careful not to slip, his thoughts as scattered as the flakes he kicks into the air. What can he do in such a short time? Maybe he could find someone at GHQ who could help ... if he had a few more days ... maybe he could move the family to some safer section of Tokyo.

If he could, he'd just stay. Resign his commission, throw his old life away. That's what he feels like doing. But that wouldn't help them. And he'd be labeled a deserter. He'd be ruined.

Maybe he should get a divorce and come back for them. But that would be too late. Anything could happen to them after he was gone.

Puffing, pushing through the cold, he glances at his watch. More than twenty minutes and he's not even at the room. He tries to go faster.

He can't solve everything, but he can do something. He hopes he can. He has to try.

Unexpectedly, Joe feels a sense of well-being wash over him. The cold drops away. The danger, the discomfort, don't matter.

Like last night at the base of Fuji, he enters a timeless zone. He feels good, oddly good.

It's like his folks during the Depression. They gave food to their neighbors; it was something they had to do. This is something he has to do. It isn't really his decision. To do anything is better than nothing, better than merely sailing away.

Joe stands a little straighter, walks a little easier, as if he forgets the sack on his back.

17

Isamu

Isamu feels betrayed. He risked everything by trying to set up a trade for his sister and by trying to help the American. Joe got what he wanted, Mama, and now he's abandoning them.

As if one door will make them safe. As if the food he gave them will keep hunger away. It's already gone. All of it.

Mama tries to calm him down.

"We'll be all right," she says.

"What will we do?"

"What we always do. Get by ... somehow," she says. "You'll see."

"I thought he was going to stay," he says.

"I did too. I was furious, but now ... I ... I just miss him."

Isamu feels another flash of hate, but he misses him too.

Not for long.

He hears him before he sees him. Clomping up the stairs. In a hurry. Other tenants probably think there's trouble, a police action. He knows it's Joe.

The steps stop outside their door and there are two hard raps. The door bursts open and the American is standing there. He swings a canvas sack onto the floor, sprinkling crystals of ice, walks to where Mama is just rising, folds her into his arms, kisses her and releases her.

He's full of energy, purposeful. He's actually smiling.

Joe squats down in front of the boy and puts a hand on each shoulder. Isamu can't avoid him, can't refuse him. He looks away, but the American cups his chin and pulls his pouty face back to the front.

"Tell that boy I have something to give him," he says.

He recognizes that Isamu doesn't understand and frowns. He

touches his cheek, holds his hand a foot above Isamu's head, holds an imaginary knife under his throat.

"Ato?" Isamu guesses and Joe nods. He points to himself and brings his hands together.

"Tell him I want to meet with him."

Isamu nods. Joe spins him around and pushes him toward the door.

"Hubba, hubba," Joe looks at his watch and makes a shooing motion.

Isamu clips down the stairs and heads out of the hotel. Where did Ato go after the Americans arrived? Probably not far. He spies a wisp of smoking coming from the warehouse.

Not far at all.

Ato is heating a can over a small blaze under one of the windows near the rear of the building. He watches Isamu walk across the large, jumbled floor.

"Looking for more trouble, Navy Boy?"

When Isamu tells him that Joe wants to see him, Ato's only question is where.

"Someplace open," Isamu says. "No surprises."

They agree on the vacant lot behind the neighborhood faucet.

This time Mama stays at home with the baby. She trades a lingering look with the American. He twists his neck to keep her in sight as he descends the stairs.

Carrying the canvas sack, Joe proceeds to the center of the lot. Ato appears with six gang members forming a line behind him. They stop about twenty yards from the American and the scarred leader comes forward.

Joe slings the bag to the ground and opens his jacket. Apparently unarmed.

He and Ato face each other across a cultural chasm of language and experience, the young officer and the defaced youth, the conqueror and the unconquered.

Joe crouches and searches inside the sack. He removes a

single shoe, then rises and holds it up.

"I give this to you," Isamu translates as Joe signs. "In return, you stay away from him." Isamu points to himself.

The American tosses the canvas at Ato's feet. He's so confident, so commanding, it's unnerving to everyone. Doesn't he understand that he's alone out here? Doesn't he remember what they did to him?

Ato kneels and inspects the contents of the bag.

"A few shoes," he sneers.

"A personal gift," Isamu translates Joe's signs. "The money you took too."

Ato stands and crosses his arms.

Joe puts his arm around Isamu and waves toward the hotel.

"I protect this boy and his family," Isamu interprets.

"We'll be here long after you're gone," Ato says and Isamu struggles to communicate it.

"The U.S. Navy protects them," Joe says.

He sneaks a peek at his watch, then points to Isamu and make a pushing gesture toward Ato. Stay away from him.

Ato faces his gang and drops his hand, evidently a prearranged signal. His cronies keep their distance, but they fan out, slowly surrounding Joe. The American calmly watches, as the boys position themselves.

"What will the U.S. Navy do about that?" Ato asks and Isamu interprets.

At another signal from Ato, the gang members show their knives or steel rods and begin, little by little, to close the circle on the American.

Joe seems assured, unafraid. He pushes Isamu to the ground. "Stay down." He reaches inside the single shoe and removes a pistol.

"Call 'em off," he gestures at the ring tightening around him.

Ato laughs and steps back.

"Can't be six places at once," he says, but Joe doesn't

understand.

Joe whirls. The other boys are edging closer. He waves the pistol at them. He thinks of the dogs when he delivered the vats of food.

Takeo flits forward and swipes at the American's sleeve, then falls back when he swings his gun toward him.

From the opposite direction, Kiro throws a knife that hits Joe's shoulder, but it doesn't penetrate the thick jacket.

Joe takes three running steps, bringing him right next to Ato. Surprised, the youth scuttles backward and falls on his butt. He pulls a knife out of his belt, but Joe kicks it away.

"Call 'em off!"

"*Fakku!*"

The American swings around and fires at the ground in front of Kiro, who's almost upon him. Kiro and the other stalkers pedal backward.

Joe straddles Ato and aims the pistol at his head. The boy is helpless. The American shoots between the scarred boy's legs, purposely missing.

Ato jumps, realizes he hasn't been hit. He smiles and kicks with all his might, tangling his legs with the American, who falls on top of him. The gun goes off.

Ato shrieks and holds his blasted knee. Pushing with his one good leg, he tries to scrabble backward.

"Joe!" Isamu yells as Takeo throws himself at the American, stabbing at his torso. Joe sidesteps and the blade glances off. The American hurls the boy away from him.

He scrambles to his feet and waves his pistol wildly, but it's unnecessary. Takeo is leaving as fast as he can.

The circle shatters. Their leader writhing in the snow, the other gang members scuttle off the lot and disappear.

Joe grabs the canvas sack, turns his back and stuffs something it, then hands it to Sam. He checks his watch again.

"I'm sorry," he mimes. "I've got to get back."

"I'll come with you."

Joe shakes his head. He coughs.

"Aiko," he says and points.

He stumbles and winces. He puts his hand to his side, where the knife struck. His jacket is ripped. Joe takes a deep breath and forces a smile, makes a short statement.

Isamu doesn't catch the exact meaning, but he gets the goodbye. He bows.

He sees red drops staining the snow as the American turns and goes.

18

Joe

He is so tired, he feels like he can't go another step, but he's got to get back. He's got to keep moving. He doesn't dare stop.

He can hardly see where he's going. It's snowing again. The sky, the ground, everything is the same soot-stained gray. This has got to be the right way.

He looks at his watch. It's stopped. Maybe he just can't read it anymore. How long before that last launch leaves the pier? How much time before they raise the gangplank?

He's got to make it. He will make it.

He slips, almost falls. That makes his chest scream in pain. He stands and tries to stop gasping, tries to breathe through his nose.

Ruins all around him. Rubble everywhere.

He goes on. Tired. God, he's so tired.

Time to sleep later. After he's back aboard. After the *Chourre* reaches open water.

He thinks of the crypto room. How many communiqués await his decoding? Anyone wonder where he is? He can picture Doc asking the other officers, "Anybody seen Binky?"

He thinks of Ato. He's glad he got to deal with him directly. He didn't mean to shoot him, but worse things have happened. It should put him out of commission for a while.

His jacket is soaked on the left side. He can tell from the smell that it's blood. He shivers in the cold.

It was worth it, wasn't it? A lot of good things occurred on this last trip into Tokyo.

He thinks of Sam, spunky Sam. Glad he stuck the gun in the sack for him. He's going to need the protection. Wish he had more ammo to give him.

Glad that he left the boy some proper footwear and that he gave Mama some additional cash.

How much time? It hurts to bring his hand up to check his wrist. Got to keep pushing.

He staggers—another slippery patch—and loses a groan no one can hear.

How long has he been out here alone? It feels like forever.

Good guys don't die like this. At any moment, Cookie and the "fellas" will appear out of the storm and rescue him.

Cold. He shakes his head to clear the flakes from his eyes.

He steps around a hole, snow covering something charred, a stick of furniture, a human? Black patterns in the white, oddly beautiful.

Will Aiko come to wave goodbye? She's like a sore tooth, a beautiful tooth, one he tongues continuously. He can't leave it alone. He can't extract it. She's part of him forever.

… her head on a pillow …

Where is she now? Where is he? He peers into swirling snow.

… the shape of her neck …

Does she suffer as much as he does? Does he want her to? Being apart is hardly bearable, but it's all they have left to share. God, how he wants to be with her.

… her hair against his chest …

It was a blessing that he came back to the room one last time. Neither expected to see each other again.

"This doesn't have to be sad," he'd said and he'd tried to sign it. He'd pointed to his eyes, indicated weeping, and shaken his head no.

She'd turned her back on him again. He thought she was still angry. But she put down the baby and spun to him. He held her for long minutes. Aiko cried softly until the boy came for him.

After that, facing Ato was easy.

He can't raise his left arm to check the time. He can't feel his left arm.

Strange, but it seems to be warming up.

He notices a building with two walls, people huddled in the only corner, watching.

He slows, breathing hard. Each step takes so much effort. He wobbles, sinks to his knees.

Tired. It's been so long since he's had time to sleep. Had time. A small cough-laugh.

He thinks of the long voyage across the Pacific. The pull of the open sea, the wave motion, the endlessness, the sense of insignificance ...

Soon San Francisco and he'll be saying goodbye to the men he went to war with ...

Then the slow train across the wide continent, rushing past the prairies, the mountains, the lakes, the towns, all the citizens proud of the American victory, all of them celebrating anyone in uniform ...

He'll have plenty of time. Sleep will heal everything.

So weary ... He lowers to all fours. His arms are quivering.

Aiko ... twenty-four hours ago. Aiko ... at this moment. What is she doing?

Someone is tugging at his shoe. His left leg. He can't move it. He can't kick.

His family is waiting, everyone eager for him, especially his wife, his little boy. It'll be good to see him ...

He feels his shoe come off. Someone is taking it, his sock too. His foot is bare and it crashes into the snow, but he can't feel the cold. His right arm won't hold ...

He teeters ... topples ...

... back to those boyhood streets, people speaking Polish, people looking out for each other. That's what he remembers. He hears his mother's voice:

"It's all right, Joey. Don't cry."

He is so tired.

"Sleep, Joey. Go to sleep ..."

About the author

Bill Baynes is a writer, producer and director. A specialist in public interest marketing, he has worked in many media formats. He was a reporter for the *Miami Herald* and the Associated Press and won awards as a documentary filmmaker. He has been active in feature film and video production, magazine publishing, public interest marketing, and website development. He has worked with school systems to create student-driven media campaigns about health-related topics.

Mr. Baynes is a member of the Historical Novel Society and the Society of Children's Book Writers and Illustrators and a board member of the California Writers Club, SF Peninsula branch, which recently honored him with its Jack London Award for distinguished service.

His young adult baseball novel, *Bunt!* was published by Silverback Sages, Abiquiu, N.M. Check out his website at www.billbaynes.com.

**TOP HAT
BOOKS**

Top Hat Books

Historical fiction that lives

We publish fiction that captures the contrasts, the
achievements, the optimism and the radicalism of ordinary and
extraordinary times across the world.

We're open to all time periods and we strive to go beyond the
narrow, foggy slums of Victorian London. Where are the tales
of the people of fifteenth century Australasia? The stories of
eighth century India? The voices from Africa, Arabia, cities and
forests, deserts and towns? Our books thrill, excite, delight
and inspire.

The genres will be broad but clear. Whether we're publishing
romance, thrillers, crime, or something else entirely, the
unifying themes are timescale and enthusiasm. These books
will be a celebration of the chaotic power of the human spirit in
difficult times. The reader, when they finish, will snap the book
closed with a satisfied smile.
If you have enjoyed this book, why not tell other readers by
posting a review on your preferred book site.

Recent bestsellers from Top Hat Books are:

Grendel's Mother
The Saga of the Wyrd-Wife
Susan Signe Morrison
Grendel's mother, a queen from Beowulf, threatens the fragile
political stability on this windswept land.
Paperback: 978-1-78535-009-2 ebook: 978-1-78535-010-8

Queen of Sparta
A Novel of Ancient Greece
T.S. Chaudhry
History has relegated her to the role of bystander, what if
Gorgo, Queen of Sparta, had played a central role in the Greek
resistance to the Persian invasion?
Paperback: 978-1-78279-750-0 ebook: 978-1-78279-749-4

Mercenary
R.J. Connor
Richard Longsword is a mercenary, but this time it's not for
money, this time it's for revenge...
Paperback: 978-1-78279-236-9 ebook: 978-1-78279-198-0

Black Tom
Terror on the Hudson
Ron Semple
A tale of sabotage, subterfuge and political shenanigans
in Jersey City in 1916; America is on the cusp of war and
the fate of the nation hinges on the decision of one young
policeman.
Paperback: 978-1-78535-110-5 ebook: 978-1-78535-111-2

Destiny Between Two Worlds
A Novel about Okinawa
Jacques L. Fuqua, Jr.
A fateful October 1944 morning offered no inkling that the lives of thousands of Okinawans would be profoundly changed—forever.
Paperback: 978-1-78279-892-7 ebook: 978-1-78279-893-4

Cowards
Trent Portigal
A family's life falls into turmoil when the parents' timid political dissidence is discovered by their far more enterprising children.
Paperback: 978-1-78535-070-2 ebook: 978-1-78535-071-9

Godwine Kingmaker
Part One of The Last Great Saxon Earls
Mercedes Rochelle
The life of Earl Godwine is one of the enduring enigmas of English history. Who was this Godwine, first Earl of Wessex; unscrupulous schemer or protector of the English? The answer depends on whom you ask...
Paperback: 978-1-78279-801-9 ebook: 978-1-78279-800-2

The Last Stork Summer
Mary Brigid Surber
Eva, a young Polish child, battles to survive the designation of "racially worthless" under Hitler's Germanization Program.
Paperback: 978-1-78279-934-4 ebook: 978-1-78279-935-1 $4.99
£2.99

Messiah Love
Music and Malice at a Time of Handel
Sheena Vernon
The tale of Harry Walsh's faltering steps on his journey to
success and happiness, performing in the playhouses of
Georgian London.
Paperback: 978-1-78279-768-5 ebook: 978-1-78279-761-6

A Terrible Unrest
Philip Duke
A young immigrant family must confront the horrors of the
Colorado Coalfield War to live the American Dream.
Paperback: 978-1-78279-437-0 ebook: 978-1-78279-436-3

Readers of ebooks can buy or view any of these bestsellers by clicking on the live link in the title. Most titles are published in paperback and as an ebook. Paperbacks are available in traditional bookshops. Both print and ebook formats are available online.

Find more titles and sign up to our readers' newsletter at http://www.johnhuntpublishing.com/fiction

Follow us on Facebook at
https://www.facebook.com/JHPfiction
and Twitter at https://twitter.com/JHPFiction